Is That Love or Fantasy?

DEVI RAGHUVANSHI was born in Mathura, INDIA, the birth place of Lord Krishna and completed his Engineering Degree (B.E.) in Electrical Engineering. After working with big Corporates for 40 years, he ventured into a writing career.

This is his ninth book, a supreme sacrifice of love and relationship, his first book "LOVE ON VENTILATOR", second book "LOVE TRIOLOGY, WHO TO COMPLAIN", third book "IT'S OK TO FALL IN LOVE AGAIN", fourth book "THE SON ROSE FROM THE WEST", fifth book "MOHINI THE TIGRESS", sixth book "LOVE LOST IN TRANSIT", seventh book "INDU THE PARCHED WOMAN" and eighth book "MOTHER VS SURROGATE (A Tale of Two Mothers)" have already been published.

DEVI RAGHUVANSHI lives in MUMBAI and he follows Sports as he himself has been a state level athlete.

He can be followed on www.facebook.com/ ds.raghuvanshi.9 or
www.deviraghuvanshi.com or
Twitter @ Raghuvanshi_DS

Is That Love or Fantasy?

DEVI RAGHUVANSHI

ZORBA BOOKS

ZORBA BOOKS

Publishing Services in India by Zorba Books, 2018

Website: www.zorbabooks.com
Email: info@zorbabooks.com

ISBN Print Book - 978-93-87456-85-3
ISBN eBook - 978-93-87456-86-0

Zorba Books Pvt. Ltd.(opc)
Gurgaon, INDIA

Printed at Repro Knowledgecast Limited, Thane

DEDICATION

Dedicated to my Parents who taught me to read and write, when they were just farmers.

This book is also dedicated to all my friends who keep reminding me to give them something different from 'Mohini The Tigress' 'Love Lost In Transit' and 'Indu The Parched Woman.' It should be similar to 'Love Triology, Who to Complain.'

Other Books Published by The Author

- Mohini The Tigress
- Love Lost In Transit
- Indu The Parched Woman
- Love Triology - Who to Complain
- **IT'S OK TO FALL IN LOVE**
- **LOVE ON VENTILATOR**
- **THE SON ROSE FROM THE**
- **MOTHER VS SURROGATE (A Tale of Two Mothers)**

ACKNOWLEDGEMENTS

I acknowledge and express my gratitude to my wife SUSHMA, for the input and spell check. All the inspiration and ideas, I conceived watching the degree of her patience.

My elder daughter PREETI deserves special mention for the emotional and financial support in publication of this book.

I would like PAYAL, my younger daughter to be a partner in this endeavour. Frankly speaking I have copied some of her blogs to make my book rich and true.

I would also express my special thanks to Mr.Rajesh Chaurasia, my colleague, for typing the entire manuscript.

Finally I thank all my friends on Facebook, my college mates, for encouraging me to write this book. My heartfelt thanks, will not be complete unless I mention the big help I got from "Bhagvad Gita' and 'Google', the boss for anything.

You all are part of my these efforts BIG or SMALL.

DECLARATION

The contents of this book are wild imaginations of the author. Any resemblance to names, places or incidences are purely coincidental and unintentional.

The author does not take any responsibility for the loss or damage to anyone on account of publication of this book except he expresses his regrets for the damage if any.

DEVI RAGHUVANSHI

1

Varun and Afreen were sitting on a railway type bench in one corner of the garden watching many people jogging and doing exercises. They were sitting talking like an young couple seeking few moments of romance away from the watchful eyes of the people that mattered to them. Varun was past mid fifth decade and Afreen could be just entering into fifth decade of her life.

It was a sheer coincidence that Afreen had brought her grand daughter with the maid in the play area of the garden for a swing and Varun was there as his normal routine to pass his time of loneliness at home. As an individual, he didn't mind spending time by himself and a lot of time he spent enjoying being alone just watching whatever he wanted or whatever he wanted to read but yes, there was time and mood where he wanted some human connection. Not that he never tried to contact several different people to just wanting any casual conversation but was left only disappointed due to his past memories hunting him and leaving a big void and vacuum to be filled.

Afreen on the other hand had a large family of four brothers, their wives and many children. Her husband Manzoor had expired seven years back due to age related problems. Afreen hardly had time to think about herself, being surrounded rather crowded by her family members. She was called Ammi, by everyone including the grandchildren. The entire family was of cosmopolitan nature far away from those typical fanatics. They were Indian first than being Muslims. They believed in being Indians first than being Muslim and following Islam. All her sons were highly educated, working for multinational IT Companies and the youngest son had a very big furniture showroom which was given to him by his father as a family business which also was doing extremely well.

Varun and Afreen never met each other since last 39 years. Afreen was fading his memory including his face whereas knowingly, unknowingly or intentionally Varun kept a close and keen watch for six years initially for everything Afreen was doing and going through pain or pleasure without she knowing it but later lost the track due to Afreen leaving the city after marriage.

What prompted Varun that day, is mystery of the unknown universe, he waited very nervously on the bench to reintroduce him to his most pleasant memories of the past, Afreen and also to know when she came back to Lucknow from Mumbai.

When Varun called out her name, Afreen spent one minute in silence with complete strangers. They just stared at each other, probably getting inspiration or energy of some sort but Varun captured Afreen's attention in a more special way because her reaction was different. Afreen came close to Varun and he introduced him to her.

Afreen almost stopped breathing for a few seconds. It turned out that the man, Varun turned out to be a 2 AM guy. It was their first time to see each other after more than 39 years and the moment was so emotional and beautiful. Love is the most wonderful thing in the world and even if some relationships don't last long due to the circumstances beyond control and the feelings fade, the memories still remain. Even though both Varun and Afreen just stood there without saying a word, they were able to speak with each other through their hearts.

Afreen to herself "why have you come back into my life after so many years? What is there between us that I should come back all the way to your life and think about you and see you." Afreen's maid was busy with the kid in the play area giving her all the rides and swings of the garden. Varun got Afreen a Choco-bar from a nearby ice-cream vendor and they both went in the flashback of their life of approx.. 40 years back. All these years they were strangers, hesitants and shy to interact. There was nothing for Varun except building fantasies of hugging and kissing Afreen.

THE MYSTERY UNFOLDS, VARUN ENCOUNTERS ILLUSIONS.

2

It was Ramadan, the holiest month of the Muslim calendar. Varun was not a Muslim but just a caring and considerate person and a very close friend of Nasir Khan. They were not only close friends but they were school and college mates too since early childhood in English medium school and College of Lucknow. During the entire month of Ramadan all the adults of Nasir's family were abstaining from eating and drinking during daylight hours and were busy carrying on their respective business as usual.

Varun one day asked Nasir whether he could also fast with him. Nasir explained to him that he could do it if he wanted to see what he felt like in doing so and it was not going to hurt his feelings in anyway but for IFTAR which is the breaking of the fast after sun down, a big communal meal, Varun should come.

Varun otherwise was also regulars at Nasir's place and knew everyone including his three brothers

Akbar, Anwar and Adil and a pretty young sister Afreen. Nasir's family also had a special liking for him.

He called up Nasir to wish him EID MUBARAK but he had gone to the Mosque for community prayer and the call was responded by Afreen. "EID MUBARAK AFREEN and BEST WISHES FROM ME TO ALL OF YOU" Varun said.

"We don't accept best wishes and EID MUBARAK on phone. We appreciate and Allah accepts wishes in person if the well-wisher is in same city." Afreen said in a cryptic tone. I would make it within one hour and even Nasir would be home by that time, isn't it?

Yes Please come.

Varun reached Nasir's house in an hour and he was welcomed by Afreen as his brothers didn't come back after the prayers. He wished her EID MUBARAK once again. She gave her a cryptic smile and said very confidently that Varun, EID MUBARAK is never done by simply vibrating your lips and saying just those two words but by hugging each other from the core of your heart.

Varun was pleasantly shocked to hear those magical words and in fact he was carried away by an exuberant, amazing and incredible beauty of Afreen. He had visited Nasir's house umpteen number of times but today, she was mischievous, a bit fervent and Varun as a Buffoon or lumpen but with an uncontrolled, unbridled euphoria. He sauntered towards a Sofa eyed by Afreen.

For Afreen, Varun was suave, charming and just perfect dude. She told Varun that actually, she deliberately told the wrong timings of her brothers coming from prayers. They were still 35 minutes left for them to come as prayers end only at 1:30 PM. Varun felt cozy and overjoyed at Afreen's telling him the lie.

Varun by nature was shy but he had a good look at Afreen from head to toes. She had the most beautiful design of Mehendi on her palms and feet. She wore multicoloured bangles in both of her hands. She was wearing fancy traditional Salwar Kameez, suitably embroidered with matching colourful shoes which was putting a spark in her personality. To complement the entire outfit, it was very important for Afreen to select accessories and right jewelry. She picked up the perfect colour and dress to enhance her beauty. It was being magnified by bold and bright colours. Afreen had infamous large typically almond shaped dark and expressive eyes with clear skin. Her hair long and lustrous black, were evidently giving him a nice tasteful sense of Aroma. She had the height and body typically like a sculptor made by the best artisans of the world. She was the most beautiful girl measured by any imaginative scales and this beauty with the dress and accessories was the most eye pleasing thing for Varun. He wished that Afreen's brothers should have done some more or long prayers. He would have absorbed Afreen in his mind, heart and soul. Afreen though didn't indicate but clearly understood that Varun had to be woken up before her brothers arrived.

Nasir came and they both hugged each other so many times and wished EID MUBARAK to all.

Varun had Sheer Khurma, Seviyan and Mutton Biryani. There were variety of desserts which he enjoyed. It was his best EID. While everyone was away to wash hands Varun thanked Afreen for a sumptuous lunch and very special moment before lunch which she reciprocated by hints from eyes and the heart. Varun thanked everyone, wished them EID MUBARAK once again and left to his house. Today was the best day of his life.

THE SEED OF LOVE WAS SOWED.

3

In all his imaginations Varun thought that he never thought it possible to love Afreen, the way he loved last night and the very thought of his love making last night in his tastefully decorated room, sent thrillers down his spine. His mother woke him up as he was getting late to go to his office. For the first time he got irritated on his mother. He picked up his towel and went to toilet. Thank you Mom, he said, smearing the thick Paratha after taking a large bite.

Varun reached his office at Hotel Clarks Avadh, Lucknow where he was working as Front Office Manager. The Hotel Clarks Avadh is a leading hotel group of India which offers an environment, perfectly designed for successful meetings and events. The hotel is situated in the city centre with aesthetically pleasing surroundings to refresh the mind featuring the spacious accommodation in any business hotel, the guest rooms and suites are planned with a host of innovative features. The rooms are designed with lot of day light offering a view of reflection of river Gomti, Swimming Pool and Landscaped Gardens.

Lucknow a capital city of Uttar Pradesh is famous for its architecture and hospitality. It is famous for its ancient monuments like Rumi Darwaza, 18th Century Imanbara Shrine. It is also called the city of Nawabi culture. People still say that everyone should go to Lucknow just to eat these eleven mouthwatering recipes, Galawati Kebab, a special delicacy, Boti Kebabs, Tunday Kebabs, Rogan Josh, Lucknowi Biryani, Tokri Chaat, Paya ki Nihari, Malai ki Gilori, Sheermals, Lucknowi Paan and Prakash ki Kulfi.

Lucknow is also rich for education, University of Lucknow, King George Medical University, Dr.APJ Kalam Technical Institute, Indian Institute of Management Lucknow, Christian College and many more speak a volume of its infrastructure of Education. Lucknow has close to 80 hotels both three to five star category like Vivanta Taj, Sarovar Portico etc.

4

Varun like a teenager felt that he has fallen in love, a situation more complex and compelling that he has known before. He was immature and was hardly understanding any aspect of love except a strong urge for sexual attraction, mutual enjoyment, emotional knowing, social compatibility, sensitive consideration, physical affection, friendship feeling and romantic excitement all combining to create a sense of caring, commitment and completeness.

There was no commitment then from either of them but Varun was having a sense of desperate attachment. It was a joy of being together coupled always with a fear of losing each other. There was always a fear in his mind whether there was any relationship between him and Afreen? What if yes, whether this love relationship at this age would survive? He never wanted to undergo break-up of this in love relationship which would become particularly painful and was fearing the hurt, helpless, betrayed, abandoned or rejected.

"Subconscious mind works in a very simplistic manner and this many times becomes the reason of misjudgments or wrong beliefs." "Varun thinks that he has not made an error of judgment regarding Afreen. Afreen is a different personality, easy go lucky type. I may have only understood her overfriendly nature as love for me."

"My mistake, I would either correct it or confirm it. I don't call it love at first sight as it never meant falling in love with Afreen after seeing her for the very first time (not necessarily having spoken to her) as Varun had met her and spoken to her many times." But if she loves me, it could only be destiny. It could be possible that something must have happened in the first meeting itself that triggered his subconscious mind into becoming attracted to her.

Yes, according to Varun, he was experiencing a combination of physical and sexual attraction, emotional intimacy and commitment. He decided to know from Afreen face to face whether she also had the same type of complications of love? or was it love or just a crush? To understand the depth of their relationship, Varun also decided to share his personal secrets and deepest inner feelings. If he found that Afreen had also experienced moments of emotional closeness with him then it might be love.

Varun strongly believed in Ramayan, a Hindu epic which says "JEHIKE JEHI PAR SATYA SANEHU, SO TEHI MILAYE NA KACHHU SANDEHU" which means that if you love someone with truth and sincerity, you will surely get him or her and there is no doubt about it.

Varun and Afreen had never been together in the past so first thing he thought of letting her know how much he loved her. Though expressing his love for the first time was quite scary but he had to be honest and open about it and he had left no option left. He made up his mind to call Afreen for lunch at Lattitude restaurant of TAJ VIVANTA, LUCKNOW which was a quiet, safe and generally happy type place for them.

Varun called up Nasir on the landline and took a chance if Afreen only picked up and to his good fortune, she only picked up.

Varun - Hi, Afreen, this is Varun. Can I talk to you for a moment?

Afreen - I could sense your call. Yes what is this call all about?

Varun - Afreen, I have something important to discuss with you in person that won't be possible on phone.

Afreen - So?

Varun - I would request you to join me for lunch in LATTITUDE, TAJ VIVANTA in Gomti Nagar tomorrow between 12 to 12:30 PM.

Afreen - You are scaring me buddy but I would join you there.

Afreen arrived at 12:15 PM and was waiting for Varun who was late by 20 minutes. She was getting restless and irritated. Varun arrived at 12:35 PM. Afreen was in a casual outfit, white top and light blue jeans with light make up. She was looking gorgeous and every passerby in the lobby was just glaring on her and some with those typical ogling eyes.

Varun after apologizing for the delay escorted Afreen to the restaurant and offered her a chair like a gentleman in one cozy corner of the restaurant. The cool open feel and stylish décor made Lattitude a lively place. Afreen liked the place and said that it is the perfect place to indulge your taste buds and in Lucknow, it is the best restaurant. They ordered Aromatized Baked Prawns and the Pan Seared Fish Fillet. Afreen had a good taste for sea food. Their discussion during lunch ranged from college to work and family affairs.

Varun — Afreen, tell me why you called me one hour before on EID when you knew very well that your brothers would be coming around 1:30 or 2:00 PM?

Afreen — Just like that. I wanted to have some fun with you which obviously, I could have not done when my brothers around. Why? You didn't like that? Then I am sorry.

Varun — No, I just loved it to be with you. In fact I felt a little uneasy on why they came so early.

Afreen — Hmm. I like it. Now tell me Varun, what's this special treat for? I understand, it's not your birthday so why the big urge to invite me today?

Varun — Just like that. Even I also wanted to have some fun with you. Frankly speaking, I like being with you.

Afreen — Why? Please for God sake, don't tell me that you started loving me that too after knowing that I have three giant brothers to protect me from these love eyes.

Varun — Honestly, I do not really know whether it is love, infatuation or a crush but I enjoy being with you.

I have had a tough time of not telling you this. I gathered three seconds of courage after taking a deep breath and counting three to blurt "I'm in love with you and I would like to spend potential lifetime of happiness with you. You are the last thought in my mind before I drift off to sleep and the first thought when I wake up each morning.

Afreen — I am terribly shocked. I knew that you have something in you which I also get attached to you, may be your this simplicity and looks but I can't gather those three seconds of courage to blurt those three magic words to you but I seem to be more matured than you to take such a big resolution at such a short instant. Give me some time to reject or accept you but don't be disappointed. My looks and my statements are some time deceptive.

Varun — I appreciate. We will meet. Remember Afreen, I can't stop thinking about you and you drive me crazy.

They ordered a special coffee which is famous for its taste and aroma.

Afreen — Bye and thanks for a nice lunch, coffee and the time, we two spent.

5

There was an international conference of tour operators and travel agents both from India and foreign countries to promote tourism and hospitality industry across the globe in October 81 at Clarks Amer, Jaipur a group hotel of Clarks Group of Hotels. Approx. 200 people were expected to attend for two days. It was to be inaugurated by Prime Minister of India. Arrangements for boarding and lodging were planned on a large scale with all minute details including room reservations, Indian and Continental recipe and the tour operators for the local sightseeing in and around Jaipur including a one day visit of Taj Mahal at AGRA.

Varun was transferred from Clarks Avadh to Clarks Amer as a single point contact for the guests and the host management. He was asked to reach Jaipur in mid-July to oversee each and everything. He reached Jaipur on July 12, 1981. He was hardly settled in staff apartments in the hotel complex only, there were very very heavy rains on July 19, 1981. All the bunds created by Rajasthan Govt. for water storage for the city, broke at the same time due to excessive rains and the heavy rains devastated entire area. The main road J. L. Nehru Road was cut to 90 feet near Malviya Engineering College and the entire water got diverted to Clarks Amer. Clarks Amer was most affected area. The floods were so heavy that the water entered in Air-conditioning Plant, Boiler Room, Laundry area, Lift wells and many other areas. It was not only water but sand running with water filled the entire basement, swimming pool and all water supplying tube wells. After the rain stopped, we could walk on the swimming pool. The engineering services were most affected as the A.C. Plant, Boiler Room, Laundry and part of electrical Switchgear, Sub-station were all damaged to a large extent.

There was some corporate meeting at Agra during this period so there was no senior person available at Clarks Amer. The entire property was cut off from all sides and even the entire communication system became out of service as the poles carrying these wires were uprooted. Varun was the only senior manager along with the Chief Engineer so all the decisions like shifting of guests to Rambaug Palace, Mansingh Hotel, making temporary arrangement of food and stay for staff were taken by him. The situation was so bad that even drinking water was not available as all the tube wells, pumps and motors were submerged in sand.

With great difficulty, Varun was able to speak to the General Manager of the Hotel in the late afternoon by using the telephonic connection of one of the shop owners and he was able to make management to understand the gravity of situation. Next day they all were there to witness this unusual site at Clarks Amer. An emergency meeting of Directors and concerned officers took place. The photographs of affected areas and machinery were taken and insurance claim was lodged. Looking into the present status, a review for the October events of October International Conference was also taken. The M.D. of the Group Hotels very clearly asked the Chief Engineer and Varun whether it would be possible to restore all services by that time. Varun after talking to the Chief Engineer, very confidently told the management that they would do everything possible to bring the hotel to its original shape and they would have the conference as per original schedule. Varun was re-designated as Officer on Special Duty for this project. It was a big responsibility.

The restoration work started. Since there was freedom to Varun to adopt ways and means, the work of the restoration was done at such a pace that Varun was able to have his first guest in the hotel within one and half months with all services. In normal course, it would have been minimum six months. The efforts of Varun and the Chief Engineer were appreciated and they both were invited for a special cocktail dinner with the Directors.

During these one and half months, Varun could speak to Afreen just once. Afreen also loved his achievements.

Varun now was a blue eyed Boy of the management and he was given sole responsibility of planning and scheduling the conference. He spoke to Afreen in the evening telling her that he was promoted as Dy. General Manager w.e.f. the day he joins back Clarks

Avadh, Lucknow after the conference at Jaipur. Her happiness knew no bounds for Varun. She only said, it needed celebration at the same restaurant in Lucknow with the same joint Chocobar. Yes "as if I don't know that you miss a heartbeat everytime, I see you. It is written all over your face."

6

Next day, his day started with a text message to Afreen "I miss you when something really good happens to me because you're the one I want to share with. I miss you when something is troubling me because you're the one who understands me so well." Actually I (Varun) was born to love you Afreen."

His message took Afreen in deep and complicated thoughts. "Varun is not only in relationship with me. He loves me truly. His love for me is like unconditional, irresistible, irrevocable, irreversible. He is someone to walk with at night and spill your life to. I hate fading away from my someone that since long is big part of my life, someone that is important to me like someone from my past birth."

"I love you Varun without speaking" Afreen said. After reading messages of each other both Varun and Afreen fell head over heel. Varun informed Afreen that he would visit Lucknow just for two days as the coming weeks would be very very busy for him due to upcoming conference. He also requested Afreen to make her available for those two days. Following Saturday, he reached Lucknow and called Afreen in Begum Hazarat Mahal Park which is an awesome place, one of the best parks of Lucknow, filled with their previous memories. The central architecture an eye catcher which makes the park inviting. One feels like sitting in the shade while watching the world pass by. This park provided them a cozy romantic corner where both of them could have had few moments all for themselves.

They stayed up the better part of the day and only got an hour or two to discuss various things related to the foreseen problems of their relationship due to their interfaith belongings. Rest of the time, there was no space even for air to enter between them.

Varun for some time forgot everything but Afreen. He loved her black big eyes. He appreciated all her little surprises like long distance calls, long distance erotic talks. She was amazed by him in a way that she always wished that Varun would be exactly like a man in her dreams and Varun also wished that Afreen would be the girl, he has always wished and fantasized. He had kindness, electrifying smile, those attractive gorgeous big black eyes and his perfect nose. By the way for Afreen, he made each of her days so much better.

They found themselves always talking about each other constantly. Varun was proud of her always supportive and loving. It finally made sense to them how a relationship was supposed to be. They were just honest with constant love. Varun walked up a bit close to Afreen and gave her a nice long hug. It was just too romantic. Though the first kiss could potentially be really awkward but he just took a natural chance and Afreen never didn't push him away which further encouraged Varun. It was absolutely Ok, to be shy the first time, he kissed her but he warmed up to her for the second time. Varun pulled his head back slowly to give Afreen some space. He wrapped a hand around her and the very next moment Afreen wrapped her hand around him and they both held each other close for a more intimate moment. He ran his hand through her hair and they remained held each other for a quiet moment.

This was the foundation stone laid for the relationship to take it to next higher level. Before leaving in the afternoon, Varun kissed Afreen's neck and pulled her close and promised to meet him tomorrow. Afreen agreed and said to Varun that you seemed like a serial kisser. Your second kiss, so passionate. We would meet for lunch tomorrow and would drop him at Lucknow Airport for his flight to Jaipur.

Next day, they met at TUNDAY KABABI, restaurant situated in a small street of Aminabad area. This restaurant is 100 years old and earned its well-deserved reputation over the years. Varun and Afreen tried Galawati Kebabs and Mutton Biryani which are really mouthwatering delicacies of Lucknow.

After the lunch Afreen drove him to the airport. The Lucknow romantic air affected their brains and bodies. The young couple had tender moments with sweet kisses. The car became a place for the couple to have their private conversations and light romance of holding hands and sharing body heat. It was like unsupervised love and romance. Both of them extended their arms around each other's shoulders and the kisses were exchanged. They parked their car in a quiet out of the way place near Lucknow Airport.

They now reached the airport for airport goodbye. Afreen just hated this goodbye specially when she was in a long distance relationship. Saying goodbye at Airport or just about anywhere was becoming something, she had to deal with. It was never easy. Then was the moment, they went into the airport. Afreen dreaded the time, in a short while, they would have their final hug which was more or less into a desperate situation like "Please don't go or go tomorrow." Varun moved and walked away, looking back, smiled sadly, waved and disappeared in the security zone after the announcement of his flight boarding.

Afreen felt empty and suddenly so lonely so was Varun. Tears were rolling down her face but there was a hope that the man, she loved, would suddenly come back. She wished that the flight was cancelled for one more day but nothing of that sort happened. She gave up and returned home.

For some time everything at home was wrong for Afreen. It was natural to feel anything right when the one, she loved like mad, wasn't with her and she couldn't feel his arms around. But yes, missing Varun so desperately was a sign that she had found something, someone very special.

7

The international conference of travel agents and other tour operators was declared a grand success and the role of Varun's untiring efforts was appreciated by one and all. He was described as a true, sincere and genuine person. He was also given Appreciation letter for completion of his project which read as under;

To,
Mr.Varun Prakash
Dy. General Manager,
Clarks Avadh Lucknow
October 01, 1981

Dear Varun,

I am writing this letter to extend my appreciation towards the successful completion of Restoration of Services of Clarks Amer, Jaipur affected by the devastating floods on time and that too with great efficiency.

I further appreciate your efforts in organizing this International Conference of Travel and Tour Operators most successfully. I really appreciate your efforts and the professionalism for the same.

I once again would like to thank you and congratulate you for your hard work and dedication.

Wishing you all the best.
Yours sincerely,
Arvind B. Gupta
Managing Director

Varun after completing all his obligations of Clarks Amer boarded a flight from Jaipur to Lucknow. He was received by Afreen with open arms.

Afreen was looking fantastic and beautiful in a new White and Pink Salwar Kameez with little make up to remind Varun of the gorgeous, well put together hottie, he left behind. She reached 30 minutes prior to his flight landing and was checking time every now and then on her wrist watch. She was so excited about him that the moment Varun came out, she made the eye contact and flashed a million dollar smile. She was so excited that once Varun was within her grasp, she made full body contact and pulled him in by his neck for a long steamy kiss. She forgot that she was in the Airport Lounge where many people were just watching her with Envy.

They drove down Lucknow roads, had hot Coffee at CCD and dropped Varun at his place without being noticed by anyone from Varun's family including his parents.

8

Varun and Afreen met at the pool side of hotel Clarks Avadh. A common friend arranged a one to one meeting between them to discuss all these issues of interfaith marriage. Both of them agreed that Hinduism is more liberal than Islam. Yes "A Hindu might be far liberal than a practicing Muslim and a Muslim might be far liberal than a practicing Hindu."

Varun - Afreen, I should have been a Muslim and you, a Hindu girl as Hindu girls have a lot more freedom in choosing their spouse as compared to Muslim girls.

Afreen - Yes, I agree and let me not mince any words or hide my true opinion on the matter. Islam is far more radicalized, conversion oriented and male dominated for the Muslim girls to be able to marry Hindu boys.

Varun - It's all a matter of personal choice. Both the people should be determined enough to confront each other's families and stay together come what may. Afreen, remember that nothing that's worthwhile comes easy. Also life is not a bed of roses.

Afreen - What's the guarantee that I would be happy marrying a Muslim of my parents' choice? Whether you marry according to your parent's wishes or your own, it takes a great deal of adjustment on your part and also on the will power to hold the relationship strong.

Varun - It's going to be long and tedious journey trying to convince our families for our marriage. We are born Hindu or Muslim not on our choice but on God's mercy so let us not change his ways. I feel we will both not convert to Hinduism or Islam. We will both follow our religions independently.

Afreen - What when it doesn't happen? You are forced by your parents to convert me in Hinduism and my parents to convert you in a Muslim. Jokingly you would look good in beard and skull cap.

Varun - Even you will look more beautiful doing Aarti and wearing typical Brahmin lady's make up. Jokes apart, if it happens we will both convert to Buddhism. Anyway we are only presuming things without even talking to our parents. Let us first give it a try.

Afreen - Ok. I will talk to my brothers and then to my parents.

They both were really very tensed but desperate to marry. Varun told Afreen that let us cross the bridge when it comes to. For the time being, let us just be two love birds. They were matured and responsible. They were worried too for the continuance of their relationship. Afreen asked Varun to discuss and resolve all issues which will jeopardize our alliance due to interfaith obligations.

All the stress between them always used to vanish when Varun used to go mad after seeing Afreen's curves and his platonic love used to go for a toss. He was working hard with him to work on him to control his urges but every time he looked on Afreen, he was a loser. Working on his nerves was more difficult than the labour he put in resolving services in Clark Amer affected by devastating floods within a record time of one and half months. Their personal tension got relieved by a tight hug and a very passionate kiss. Her body contact with Varun made him go over the moon and so was Afreen. She melted faster than the icecream. What an encounter!.

9

Afreen discussed this issue with her brothers. They were initially under a thunder shock. They were neither supportive nor being so aggressive to stop her marrying Varun, a Hindu boy. Nasir supported her but his opinion carried no weight to convince their father. The father was very angry, shell shocked and disturbed and his first reaction was a BIG NO. After sometime, he said that marrying Varun is not only the relationship between you and him, it is the relationship of two families that are 180 degree apart in religion, customs and followings. We have our reservations that this marriage would involve the healthy and interacting families. Religions are made for a purpose or reason and marrying in other religion can jeopardize an existence of religion in you. Afreen was sadly disappointed. She thought .... My father though a devout Muslim, was liberal in the sense that he educated us in English medium schools. I graduated in Journalism and pursuing management. All my three brothers are employed in Multinational IT Companies and the youngest in a Furniture business and Fashion World. Here I have fallen in love with Varun, a typical U.P. Brahmin and this has already taken deep roots in my life. Initially I was indifferent to him though he is very attractive, well settled. His interaction has always left a big impression in my heart and soul. He is very smart and intelligent, yet very humble and soft spoken. We started spending more time together. Initially our love was like a slow race in slow motion but now I have fallen in love so deep that if some other girl talked to him smilingly or flirted with him, I feel the pangs of jealousy. I am becoming possessive and want him just for me. He knows it and always reciprocates my feelings admitting that he is madly in love with me too.

We two were afraid to commit because of our different religions and he has already had a tragic prior-experience of an inter-religion marriage in his family. Varun is very clear since day one that he never wanted me to change religion. In fact now we both have decided to continue to practice our respective faiths while supporting each other whenever possible. Varun has promised to keep ROZAS (FAST) with me and I have promised to fast for him on KARVA CHAUTH (a Hindu Festival) but the problem was with our families. Upon Varun's insistence his parents have agreed for our marriage but his other relatives are vehemently opposing it. This has made his parents a bit reluctant.

Now my father and two brothers have stopped speaking to me for Hindu alliance especially being a Brahmin. Nasir was always supportive but again his views are not taken seriously by anyone of them though he is my only hope. My biggest problem is that I never wanted to leave Varun and neither I wanted to leave my family. I have tried to convince my father a lot that I am not reneging on my faith but he finds my decision to marry outside my religion unacceptable. I started exploring the ways to marry a Hindu while still being a Muslim. Is there any way out to convince my father? Or is it that I have to sacrifice on one of them, Afreen felt that if she is to leave Varun, she would end her life because living without Varun is looking rather impossible.

My brothers and close relatives have advised me that it is better for me to forget love and make Allah and my dad happy because I belong to them and I owe them a lot. They are the ones who gave me life and support and request me not to rebel against them. In the worst circumstances, I have to ask Varun to accept Islam against my conscience.

Varun and his friends have advised me to go ahead with this marriage. They have told me that there is a special marriage process for interfaith marriages like ours in our country. Some of them even said to me that even if I get converted to Hinduism, I can still continue with my faith. Varun always asked me not to convert to Hinduism. He has told me that I would have all the freedom as a woman to think and act as I wanted. I had a classmate in my college. Heena Khan, a close confidante for any emergency who told me that true Islam only says about love and forgiveness. It is not mandatory to change religion for the sake of marriage. Ok, when it comes to children, you can leave it to them what they want to follow as pure conclusion of every religion is same.

Some English friend of Varun was very clear in his mind who asked me to try to grow up and expand my mind and see the world and things beyond religion. God is merciful and kind and he doesn't bother about which religion the boy is from so long as he is a good human being. He advised me to have a mature adult conversation with my dad and make him understand that religion would not be more important than humanity. Forcing Afreen to change Varun's religion is also not right.

10

This happened then in Sept'83 and later around October, her parents forced Afreen to accept a proposal from their community. Afreen was being forced to marry someone by her parents. This guy Manzoor who, she was being married was more educated and wealthy than the one Varun who she wanted to marry. Manzoor was working in Mumbai and was 12 years older than Afreen. Afreen kept on asking Varun what she must do? "Shall we elope?" Varun never approved the idea of eloping but to wait. For few days they both avoided each other, neglecting each other's feelings but somehow were not able to resist it. Varun through texts or messages to Afreen told that he has once again got mad about her. Varun met her and saw that she was very depressed as she never wanted to marry Manzoor. Her mother also coerced her, threatened her and did what not but Afreen vehemently told her mother that she loved Varun and would get married to him only.

Afreen's parents were trying a forced marriage to this business man of Mumbai which she never wanted and to marry Varun, she didn't have consent from her parents and brothers. Every trick like coercion, guilt, threat, blackmail, harassment, financial pressure, emotional pressure, physical violence, psychological duress were tried. But Afreen didn't budge. She was beaten up by parents and her brothers.

At one point of time Afreen wanted to take legal action and leave her parent's house but again Varun didn't agree for this and asked Afreen not to go for legal action. After all they are your own and you can't afford to fight with your parents, though that was a clear case of domestic violence act against her parents and brothers wherein a Magistrate can pass an interim order of restraining the people from forced marriage. Afreen had many options to protest like contacting National Commission for Women – Does a father have right to marry her daughter against her wish according to Islam? She knew that Islam treats men and women equally in regards to the right to choose a mate. It has not given parents any such authority.

Her parents have disapproved of her choice for not being a Muslim and this guy was a Muslim also. Afreen did not accept their verdict and also she never wanted to follow this route of legal action or reporting to National Commission for Women. She always tried to convince her people to agree for her marriage with Varun. Afreen even gave ultimatum to her parents that she would not marry anyone other than Varun even if she had to stay unmarried. Even Varun told her that he would marry Afreen with full consent of her parents. He set up a time line of 1 to 2 years to convince all. Really it required a lot of sensitivity.

When Afreen's parents couldn't convince her they asked her to meet the man at least once. She with no interest met Manzoor. He looked obsessed with her as she was beautiful and polite. Afreen watched that man for 4-5 days and noticed that he was spying on her phones, e-mails and chatting applications. Finally out of frustration, she refused to marry him.

Both Varun and Afreen agreed to have at least a go full throttled for convincing them. Afreen was low in self-esteem/confidence. This time it was Varun who wanted to have one to one face off with Afreen's father.

Afreen was very happy when Varun told his resolve to meet her father and try his best to put the house in order failing with they would elope, get married, and may what come. There was a sudden change of everything between them. The chemistry between them started doing some adult chain reactions. Hormonal changes triggered by brain and body developments were strongly implicated in the intense feelings of sexual attraction and falling in love. Testosterone and Oestrogen male and female sex hormones were associated with heightened sexual urges and it became difficult to control the desires. For the first time, they united in body and soul without any guilt.

11

Varun met Afreen's father and sought his blessings to marry his daughter Afreen. He immediately asked Varun to first convert to Islam. Varun told him that they both are not interested in conversion. Mehboob Miyan, Afreen's father annoyingly told Varun, "you have two choices, first leave Afreen and get lost forever, never ever to be seen close to my daughter, second, convert to Islam then we might favourably consider your alliance with my daughter." Varun said, "Abba, this caste, religion are made by humans, love is created by God and it is considered to be sacred." I can only tell you that I love Afreen irrespective of caste and all. Afreen is also on the same frequency of conversation. Afreen loves you all so she doesn't want to offend you but the fact remains that she wants to marry me as Afreen and not a converted Hindu woman. Ideally I feel, it is her responsibility to convince you, the way I have done it with my parents.

Varun, Islam doesn't allow us to marry Afreen to you without converting to Islam as Hindus are considered as non-believers. Abba, I am not an authority to challenge your statement on Islam but whatever I have read and learned from Afreen, I will have to tell you that;

- Forced conversion is a sin in Islam.
- A conversion will be valid only if you believe in one God (Allah) and in Prophet Mohammed being his messenger. Otherwise, it is just Blasphemy.
- Can you assure me Abba, that I will make a better husband if I accept Islam and not otherwise?
- Can you assure a happy future for your daughter with another Muslim man especially when your daughter is in love with me? Don't you think, it will spoil three lives.
- The Special Marriage Act law in India was made to facilitate interfaith marriages and our's is a perfect case.

Afreen's father was flabbergasted and speechless but he still resisted it with lot of patience to deal with all the opposition and negativities from his family, friends and the society. He argued that Religion and faith is a very private and personal thing. No one can force upon you and me. It's good for you and Afreen to understand this and support me. Varun never wanted to fuel his EGO and left him with a promise to come again and try to bring out real moderate Muslim in him.

Varun was not very happy but was not lost on hopes. He was not disappointed. At least he was happy that Afreen never asked him to convert. Afreen was knowing that it will create intense relationship problems between both of them in future.

12

They did not listen to her and decided to go ahead with their decision. Afreen and her parents informed Manzoor, the prospective bridegroom from Mumbai about her past relationship. He was cool and said that it was her past and would not think about it. Afreen under the circumstances, had no option but to elope with Varun and she told this to Varun. Varun said, "Our brains work 24 hours a day, 365 days a year .... right up until we fall in love. We have been in love but would or should not be so crazy in love that we can do anything, right from eloping, to committing suicide to killing someone though we both are experiencing just that." Varun further said, "Every love story does not have a happy ending and every romance also doesn't end on sweet note. I know that love hurts." Do we want to lose the battle without fighting? We still have time and mental resources. We will still explore them and convince them to accept our marriage. What did you achieve after meeting my father except insults and humiliations? Afreen demanded. Ok that was as expected. Now Afreen, you speak to your father for the last time and after that if he doesn't accept us, we would elope.

Next day, she met her father and expressed her last desire that she is thinking of calling herself as spiritual not religious. Allah has created the EARTH and the HEAVENS, PLANETS and the SYSTEM and programmed them to function cohesively then why not Varun be included in our family without being converted?

Iqbal — We will but he has to convert to Islam.

Afreen — But I do not want him. I would rather convert to Hinduism and follow Islam at his place.

Iqbal — What about other rituals like Sunat (Religious circumcision)?

Afreen — Our kids will be either Hindus or Buddhists and then there is no question. I personally hate our system of FGM (Female Genital Mutilation) for young girls. It's so painful and unhygienic. I would not have allowed you or anybody even if I would have married a Muslim of your choice.

Iqbal — In that case, we do not accept Varun as our Son-in-law.

Afreen — One more thing Abba, I would like to clarify few more things;

- Varun will not convert to Islam.
- Children born to us will have mostly Hindu names or at the most Buddhist names.
- Our children will not undergo SUNAT.
- I may do idol worship.
- I'll also start putting Bindi and apply Vermilion

Iqbal   - Then you forget about everything. I will marry you with Manzoor come what may.

Afreen   - You may do so at the cost of losing your daughter.

Iqbal   - It would be worth sacrificing you rather than going against tenets of Islam.

Afreen   - Last thing Abba, I will either marry Varun or nobody come what may.

There wasn't a common platform to meet for either of them and they both departed with their individual resolves let us see who succeeds.

13

Eloping seems easy but leaves scars on lives of our parents and our people. Starting from our own friends, some of them would be hurt by our secret engagements and elopement. They would be surprised and could like the excitement as they think they would be part of all our celebrations. Some of them would also comment "OH HOW EXCITING! THEY FOLLOWED THEIR HEARTS. THAT'S LIKE MEGA SUPER AWESOME."

Varun further continued to Afreen ....

For the parents it would be a shock of life time. They would be heart broken, depressed beyond limits of repairs. The society around our parents is so cruel that they would only find faults and would start mudslinging and will not waste even a minute in slut shaming.

Afreen, tomorrow, we would also have kids, a boy or a girl or both what would be our fate then? Let us think a little bit about it and decide. It doesn't mean that I am dragging feet out of fear of being ostracized or decapitated but I am of the belief that all is not lost now. We would again fix up a time line of say one year. We would be 28 and 27 years after one year. Afreen initially was furious at his idea and was even prepared to say FUCK OFF to Varun but wise sense prevailed and she understood that Varun is a much better human being than that she knew so far. He is not thinking only about us but even about our parents. He forewarned Afreen that after eloping, and getting married, we have to face them and we would not be in position to derive true happiness after we see grief or hate into their eyes. You love them and let us ensure they love us in all conditions and all times.

Afreen hugged him tightly and kissed him so many times before he found it hard even to breath.

14

Iqbal Khan and his family tried their best to dissuade their daughter Afreen from marrying a non-believer of Islam, Varun, a Hindu boy and their seven years long relationship had sparked vehement opposition from relatives. The entire family was feeling humiliated by their daughter's behaviour and viewed the relationship as an affront to the family's honour. Iqbal and his sons tried to intimidate Afreen into dumping her boyfriend. He even threatened Afreen that he would spend his whole life in jail if he has to kill Varun for this reason.

He talked to his friends including some Muslim Khap Panchayat of Western U.P. "LOVE MARRIAGES ARE DIRTY .... ONLY WHORES CAN CHOOSE THEIR PARTNERS" was the statement of one of the council leaders of that Muslim Khap Panchayat. In such environment, a woman who refuses to enter into an arranged marriage will be viewed by the Khap as having dishonoured them so grievously that her male relatives would be ostracized and their siblings will have trouble finding suitable spouses. Killing her the only way the family can restore its honour.

Though neither Islam nor Hinduism directly sanctions killings but both play a role in legitimizing the practice. Iqbal got scared and decided not to use their services. He was a moderate Muslim.

He discussed with his sons about his discussion with his friends and Khap members without revealing his intent.

Varun as usual was busy in his work and in efforts to keep the rebellion under control. He was not aware of the plans made by the henchmen and Iqbal Khan through Khap Panchayat to illegally abduct Varun and forcibly drag him to some unkown place with a sole purpose of dissuading him to love Afreen, humiliating and coercing his parents with a threat of killing him and the entire family.

Varun initially was told that he is going to meet Afreen who was injured in a bike accident near her college. The accident was big but she survived. The four people claimed to be staff members of her college. They also informed Varun that Afreen's family was already there. Without giving it an iota of suspicion, Varun sat in their Mahindra SUV500 and they drove him first towards Afreen's college then towards a route to Nepal. The SUV had dark glasses so nobody from outside was able to see through. When Varun protested, he was first threatened then made unconscious by using a cloth soaked in Chloroform.

When after few hours, Varun regained senses, he was asked to climb out into a dry hot day and walk to the front door of another car. Mahindra SUV was not permitted to enter beyond this point. He moved towards the doorway of low ceilinged house, half built, with green coloured curtains on doors and windows. From some distance, it looked like a small rural dispensary. Varun was asked to follow in the adjoining room, Varun thought that he wouldn't stay long. It was nice of one of the guys to offer Varun a soft drink and some snacks.

Varun asked the leader of the gang, what was the reason for him being here? Have I been kidnapped? If yes then why and who had done it? What were my stakes? The man in blue shirt and black trousers with fearsome red eyes, six feet tall, long haired, a typical of Hindu movie type kidnapper said, "You are kidnapped, you are in a different country. What is to be done, when you will be released or not, I am not aware of it."

"We have to keep you safe for few weeks and further action will be communicated to us later." "You would not be harmed, if you behave but in case you try to run away then, we have been advised to kill you and dump your body in the jungle right in front of you."

After a day Varun was moved towards the adjoining Bungalow which looked like deserted for a long time where civilization has not reached. Varun was taken to a room. There was no air. He was asked to occupy a cot. "A man turns his gaze from the wall, sees Varun and murmurs No, No, No, bald partially, fragile with bones of his face so thin, thick black lips, opens his mouth and asks Varun, you are so good looking man, you can get 100 Afreens. Why don't you leave one belonging to Iqbal Bhai. Leave her. For the first time, I want to become a human. I don't know why? But I don't want to kill you. You are a Brahmin so BRAHMHATYA (killing to Brahmin) should not be done. You have time and chance to think. I will be away in these dense forests for few days and please tell me after I am back. You will otherwise not be able to even to see the dead bodies of your kins."

Varun understood the entire mystery of the episode and told that man that he had no smile or appropriate facial expression of fear to offer you. " I am sorry for the efforts you have made to silence my voice but please understand, I love Afreen." "They are useless words irrelevant. We have been given a specific task and are paid for the same. If you coolly walk off from the scene of Iqbal and Afreen saga, we won't harm you otherwise you know what could be done. Your countdown has started now."

15

Varun's father lodged a police complaint in Imambara Police Station for his son allegedly having been kidnapped and they were having no clue about his whereabouts. They had already searched him everywhere including his friends' places, hospitals etc. He may have been brainwashed to convert to Islam. They gave police a possible clue about his affair with a Muslim girl. They also lodged a missing person's complaint about their son.

When Afreen came to know about Varun's kidnapping, she raised her voice against her father and brothers then the hell broke loose on her. She was beaten up by her family. She was put on house arrest and threatened. When Afreen asked her father why this was done to Varun, his first reaction was to show ignorance of the incident but on persistent asking he said that he deserved it. He did not accept to leave you and left no option with us except that he had to be kidnapped and kept away from you. He kept on repeating that all that he wanted for, was having you as his love life. Till last he kept on convincing us for the marriage without any one of you being converted. We explained and told him to leave you but we found him a hard nut to crack so we threw him back like a ball hitting a strong wall to the kidnappers.

Nasir was always a supporter of Afreen and Varun but being the youngest son, he could not help his sister. He told Afreen that Dad had arranged a SUPARI (Contract Killing) for kidnapping Varun and killing him in case he didn't leave you. While he was kidnapped, he resisted too much but finally silenced by putting a cloth soaked in Chloroform on his face. He was also forcibly fed something and within minutes, he felt immense heat in his body and lost his conscious within no tome and fell on the car seat. (This is what I heard dad telling Ammi). Now dad would come and ask you for the last time if you wanted to save him and get married to Manzoor. In case you didn't agree then Varun would be killed by the same kidnappers. "Afreen, I suggest, you agree to whatever he says and save Varun, after all you loved him, he loved you and he is my childhood friend."

Afreen was placed in the saddest state of mind. She now understood that a Hindu guy marrying a Muslim girl with parents' approval was way tough than what one could imagine. Afreen now was waiting for her father to come and negotiate Varun's life. How would she react, she didn't know only God knew.

A little later Iqbal Khan came and started his judgmental verdict like a Supreme Court judge. "Under Shia Law, no Muslim male of female can marry a Non-Muslim in NIKAH form and we would not accept your marriage under the SPECIAL MARRIAGE ACT 1954. You are aware that Varun has refused to convert to Islam.

"Afreen, now you have two choices;

1) Forget everything about Varun as if nothing has happened. If you accept that we would marry you immediately to Manzoor and Varun will be saved and brought back to Lucknow, the day you leave for Mumbai.

2) If you don't accept it, you will be a big loser. You will lose Varun for life and you will have no relationship with our family.

So think you have exactly 24 hours to revert. In any case, we have decided to marry you with Manzoor at whatever cost."

Afreen   - "If that is like this, then why are you asking me?

Iqbal   - Just to give you an opportunity to think for a peaceful marriage."

Afreen under some mysterious circumstances gave her consent to marry Manzoor. Preparations got underway on lightning speed.

16

In India, sacrificing their relationship to accept parent's decision is a common phenomenon and Afreen was no exception to this and she unwillingly agreed to by her parents' wish of marrying Manzoor and leaving Varun and his hopes of garlands, bangles and vermilion.

"Varun loved me to the Moon and back so did I. Now that a piece of my heart is always missing you when you are not with me. The feelings of inadequacy is running so deep within me that I end up feeling ashamed. I don't want to be termed as selfish lover which I am not but in the situation since your life could be jeopardized, I am becoming a selfish lover and would like to leave you to marry someone else. Since we love each other, I would need you to do these things for me as a promise to have loved me or love me now."

I know, it will take a lot of time to draw me out of you but................

- Find out other places to invest your loving energy besides me, this will reduce your own torture.
- Confront your own pain and recognize things that you need to develop. This would relieve you of your feelings of emptiness.
- Don't let your anger get the better of you but at the same time don't pretend not to be angry or sad.
- If it can, please settle down in life and get married for the sake of my happiness. The family would drag you to a happy life.

Last but not the least, Varun please, please, please Don't let your emotions drive your decisions or your behaviour.

We may not meet again but this might give me some strength to move on in life.

We now part ways on unconditional love which by virtue of religions was not grounded on healthy foundations.

We both would respect some wise man's advice as ....

THE UNFORTABLE TRUTH : ALL RELATIONSHIPS END EVEN IN LONG TERM MARRIAGES, ONE OF THE TWO DIES BEFORE THE OTHER LEAVING THEIR PARTNER IN DEEP GRIEF.

BYE AND GOD BLESS YOU.

(This was a small handwritten note of Afreen handed over to Nasir, to be handed over to Varun)

17

Aftab Manzil, Afreen's house was the centre of the attraction. It was a day Khans waited for. Decoration of the house was started from the entrance door because all the relatives and guests are going to flow through entrance. New curtains with strings of white lights and Jasmine flowers were fixed. The entry way could not have been more pleasant and charming than this.

The entire bungalow was tastefully lighted up with a generous amount of lighting and Diyas were placed all over to cover the entire area including the staircases. The trees outside the Bungalow were decorated with tiny multi-coloured lights of green and blue combination and the tree leaves and branches were focused by using uplighters. The entire house itself was looking like a bride. There was light music through piped routes. The guests started pouring in and there was joy and happiness in every nook and corner of the house. Everyone in the house was in celebration mood and on cloud nine except Afreen who was maintaining a mysterious stoic silence. Only she could read the contours of pain and agony in her heart and Nasir was the only person who was sharing it. Everyone else in the wedding seemed to be very happy and jolly including the parents of Afreen in excitement but she was looking very sad and discontent. Nobody saw the tears of Afreen and she never wanted to show also. A wedding day is supposed to be one of the happiest days of couple's life but the sadness on Afreen's face when standing in the group in her wedding dress appeared to have told a different story which nobody noticed. Her sadness was generally taken as a traditional shyness on bride's looks but one very close friend, Nilofer noticed this sadness and unspoken fear and uncertainty even when she was in her room with her friends before the ceremony or at the parlour. Afreen was completely withdrawn and quiet. Even in this state, she was looking most beautiful, covered with her internal turmoil. She was to save her love come what may.

Muslim weddings are simple, alluring and elegant. Both Muslim men and women around the world follow specific laws and practices laid down in Quran. These weddings rituals extend up to three days. The colourful themes are followed in different parts of the world depending upon local traditions. Besides bride and groom, relatives friends and family members enjoy the whole treat with different rituals.

Afreen followed all rituals religiously starting from SALATUL ISHTIKARA to THE CHAUTHI CEREMONY.

Muslim weddings are known as NIKAH in Urdu. The traditions or rituals differ according to region, sects and customs of people involved but down the line, every wedding has one significant purpose to it, celebrating the sacred union of two people and two families.

THE ISHTIKARA RITUAL – This is the most important ritual in a NIKAH. The religious heads of the Muslim community come together to pray to Allah and seek his consent and blessings to commence the wedding.

THE IMAM-ZAMIN RITUAL – In this ritual, the groom's mother visits the bride's house bringing sweets and a gold or silver coin wrapped in a silk cloth. She ties this cloth around bride's hand.

THE MANGNI – This is also called engagement ceremony, during which the boy and the girl exchange rings. Both the families exchange gifts, fruits, dry fruits and sweets.

THE MANJHA RITUAL – During this ritual, the bride wears yellow clothes and paste made out of turmeric is applied on her face and body. After this ceremony the bride is not supposed to leave her house until the wedding day.

THE MEHENDI – This is same as Hindu ceremony. In the Mehendi ceremony beautiful and artistic henna designs are applied or bride's hands and feet.

THE SANCHAQ RITUAL – In this ritual, the groom's family sends clothes and ornaments for the bride to wear during NIKAH.

RECEPTION OF THE BARAAT – The bride's family welcomes the baraat (wedding party) with welcome drinks and gifts. The groom then shares a glass of

SHERBET (a sweetened drink) with the brother of the bride.

THE NIKAH – This is the main ritual or actual wedding ceremony and is conducted in presence of Maulvis (religious priest) and close family members from both families. According to traditional and religious customs, men and women sit separately. The bride is given a MEHR (a pre-decided amount of cash given to the bride) from the groom's family. The religious priest recites prayers from Queen and asks the bride if she agreed to marry the groom. This question is asked thrice and the same is repeated with the groom. This is known as proposal and acceptance. This is followed by signing the NIKAHNAMA (Marriage Contract) by the couple. All the elders now bless the newly married couple.

THE ARSI MUSAF RITUAL – This is the time when the newly married couple gets to see each other for the first time after marriage.

THE RUKSAT RITUAL – The bride bids a tearful farewell to all her family members after all the wedding ritual have taken place. On her arrival at Groom's house, the bride is welcomed by Groom's mother with the Holy Quran placed on her hand.

THE WALIMAH – A grand and lavish reception feast, also known as DAWAT-E-WALIMAH, is organized by the groom's family. This is a way to welcome a new member in the family and also to make a formal announcement of the marriage to the entire community.

THE CHAUTHI CEREMONY – This ceremony is basically a lunch or a dinner organized by the bride's family when she visits her house for the first time after marriage with her husband. They are given lot of gifts.

Afreen unwillingly performed all the rituals and left Lucknow to Mumbai, her husband's place. For her, this wedding had made her life miserable. It was like either a forced marriage when Islam does not support in any way a marriage where either the man or woman is unhappy with the setup.

In spite of lot of problems between Afreen and the entire family she was the most loved child of the parents and the darling sister of all brothers. For her mother it was the most painful moment of her life. She had given her daughter everything. Departure or Rukhshat of her daughter was a very touching moment of this wedding for everyone present there. "She now belongs to someone else, her husband she will not be able to say Good morning Ammi, good morning Abba every morning. She will be away from their personal love and affection. She will not have those loving and angry arguments." Iqbal wept like a child and regretting his beating and abusing her and asked Allah to forgive him. Though they all had hopes for her happiness on her joining her husband to start a successful new life.

Nobody knew the extent of pain, Afreen was going through. She was all the time feeling like a sacrificial goat. Afreen soon started feeling the blues, commonly referred as post wedding depression an emotional response to the withdrawal. She reached Mumbai by evening flight.

18

After three weeks Varun was moved out of that place to the road and back into the car. Everyone in the car was silent. Varun also didn't ask anyone what happened to them now? Varun was taken to another house for a day and next day in another car with Indian registration number mostly fake. He was covered with a blanket and they took him somewhere. Varun's breath was caught in his throat and he couldn't speak now. Semi-unconscious, he was left off at the same place where he was picked up from three weeks ago. Those people disappeared along the border between India and Nepal.

Varun reached home and needed urgent medical aid against trauma and depression.

19

Varun came back home from trauma centre and got another shock of Afreen leaving Lucknow after having married. He returned to his previous state of mind whatever good or bad sentiments may happen. He asked his parents to withdraw all complaints of his kidnapping and missing.

Arriving home alone had a pain of his own. Varun felt everything wrong. How could he feel anything right when the person he loved more than he himself, wasn't with him anymore, like he couldn't hear her voice, couldn't hear her footsteps any more, couldn't feel her arms around his shoulders. Nothing made sense for Varun. There was an empty feeling almost as if someone had died or like he himself had lost part of him. Varun was continuously crying. There was no cure for this final goodbye.

Break up was not a fun. Nasir informed Varun against his father's wishes that Afreen married Manzoor to save your life and also handed over a handwritten note of Afreen to Varun. Afreen had given her tips for creating a less painful ending for Varun. Varun was not prepared for this as this had become so sudden and quick that left him reeling from sudden pain and shock. He made up his mind to make it possible to leave Afreen and keep his heart and dignity intact. He was feeling angry, hurt and betrayed like a victim but again he remembered Afreen's words that instead of feeling angry or victimized by the circumstances, he looked at the silver lining in his relationship and not to grieve. He also resolved that after leaving his lover, he would love himself back to life assuming and experiencing that there is an abundance of love in the world just waiting for him and closing the doors to a relationship that no longer exists. He resumed at Clark Avadh as usual.

After Afreen left, Varun allowed himself a bit of time just to be miserable but he always felt a need of Afreen to come back but Afreen was 1500 Kms away from him.

How long would be brood about it?

Afreen truly loved him. She is married to someone else due to some unfortunate reason. Will she remember him and her past? Yes, she would because it was true love and a real time incident that happened in their lives but again how often is she going to think about him? A loss is a loss however small but the wound heals. She would be remembering him but not in that longing way again. After all he also has to move on in life.

Varun only hopes that if she is married to someone else, she will have a long successful happy life with him. For me (Varun) it is time to get over her and go spread the love around. True love on one side and getting married under family pressure on other hand is quite a strange and complex situation to deal with but Afreen must have gone under maximum stress to agree. She must have fought till last before she must have given up.

When Nasir informed Varun about the circumstances, under which Afreen agreed to marry Manzoor, it disturbed Varun emotionally and physically to a large extent. Whatever has happened to this man, life has added a new feeling to the memory box in his mind that would keep coming back and forth as his life moves on without any prejudice towards Afreen and her family. Varun knew that After breakup a serious relationship, it takes a while to move on but you can't erase it from your memory ever plus he has the moral support in form a piece of paper written by Afreen that was handed over by Nasir to him.

Varun resumed his work at Clarks Avadh and forced him to get lost in so much of work so whenever he found anything that made him remember Afreen, the feelings got strong and images or instances ran in his mind as flashback, he put himself to be too busy in other activities. As the days were passing, Varun realized that the thought about Afreen has not crossed his mind. He tried to think that the life is too pleasant and beautiful and he would be rude if he won't spend it smiling. He also anticipated that Afreen's marriage is successful than all her old memories would be erased and written all over with the new one. She is an intelligent and affectionate girl so she would need few weeks to get along and few months to get adjusted to new life.

In life, change is permanent so as the days pass by, everything would be forgotten. She might have few moments of life to remember but even that would fade away. It is surely not impossible to live happily in a marriage and neither is it impossible to move on from her past.

Varun promised to himself that he would abide by everything, Afreen wished except he would not marry and fall in love again. Afreen sitting 1500 Kms away was not aware of Varun resolutions. She was all together in a different world which Varun was not aware of.

20

Afreen has been married for four years now but she has never slept in the same bed as her husband's with consent. Whatever, however and whenever this has happened, it was always under brute force from Manzoor. It was always a bloody cruel rape. Manzoor says, "he loves her but Afreen thinks that this is just misguided Indian Muslim talking about of pride and honour."

Afreen was like a child, innocent but bonded with big dark eyes under some sort of fear. Sometimes in those moments in the dining room, Manzoor would prelong conversation which implied that he wanted to sleep with Afreen. Afreen usually used to get nervous but a mental strength was developed beneath Afreen's physical fragility. She used to leave him, got food for herself and went to other room bolted it from inside as she was always scared because she was a tiny sophisticated female and Manzoor this big tall guy.

Out of these forced rapes, Afreen gave birth to a male child who looked different than other kids. He always looked unhappy and felt lost. Afreen was confused and always thought, "what to do? The kid was always a reminder of a violent attack by Manzoor. Her confidence was destroyed because her child's deviant behaviour was genetic. She was always worried by thinking that Evil was embedded in his genes and people could tell somehow that the kid has been created from violent rape and not out of consensual union. She went on scratching her brains that even he could be a rapist in future.

Shaken on nerves, Afreen started looking after him patiently and giving him proper medication but a great sadness flooded through her always. One very famous doctor from Bombay Hospital told Afreen after examining her kid that he would most probably suffer from severe psychological disorder, the most common is Post Traumatic Stress Disorder (PTSD), depression and anxiety. He might face many challenges now in life.

Afreen informed Manzoor about the health of their son, he didn't react like a father. He blamed Afreen's genes for the same which put the final nail in the coffin and whatever little hope of continuance of their relationship remained was dashed to pieces. Even the child of three years started feeling that he was never meant to exist. Sick and irritated all the time.

Manzoor was hardly present when his son was growing. He never carried out the duties of fatherhood diligently. He was losing temper and behaving badly not only with Afreen but with the kid too. He always forgot that one day his son would follow his example. Sometimes, he was also physically violent with beating, teaching his son that aggression was one way of dealing with conflict. He was not only criticizing his wife but at times, he was finding unnecessary faults in his son and was generally blaming Afreen for the upbringing. He was mostly detached from the family and the sole blame game was on Afreen. She many times thought that it was better to end something and start another than to imprison yourself in hoping for the impossible.

Afreen's son, one day was reported to be having constant cough and cold, when he was taken to the hospital, the doctors detected a chronic case of Pneumonia and his health was continuously deteriorating. She practically begged for help from her husband but he only attended his kid in the hospital but there was no word of sympathy towards Afreen. This Pneumonia was followed by diarrhea and he started losing on breath. He was put on ventilator support system. The baby suddenly came down with fever. The child fought the battle but lost on life.

The death of her child was the single most traumatic event and for Afreen it was like losing a piece of herself. There was no tragedy in life like the death of her child. Things never got back to her to the way they were when her child was with her. Now she was seriously struggling in her marriage. She thought that she needed to get a divorce because she disliked her husband so much. Now the hate for her husband became bigger than the grief of losing her son. Manzoor in spite of the tragedy was still thinking that her way of doing things was not the right way and there was complete disconnection from each other's feelings. Manzoor now was not taking care of Afreen. Afreen lost all her patience and decided to end her relationship with Manzoor or could be with her parents and brothers. So much of hate and venom she had for them and an immeasurable grief for herself.

21

The pressure on Varun to marry was mounting by the parents, specially his mother using too many emotional quotes. He was trying to explain to them that he has had a stagnant relationship few years back when he was to marry and suddenly things came to an end. It has hurt him and made him difficult to come of it. If I marry now, I am more scared to hurt my feelings again. Varun was explaining to his parents and relatives that the relationships are extremely fragile and can break due to unrealistic expectations, simple misunderstanding and minor issues and once it breaks like my last one, the task of restoring it will be challenging. Trying to get the same intensity as before is not only hard but takes a lot of time, consistency and patience. For me, since I am living in NO HOPE region so making new relationship looks herculean task.

Varun's father explained to him that your last relationship became a victim of circumstances or accident. It is never necessary that things repeat again, what is needed of you is your renewed commitment to yourself and the new partner to be good and in resonance to each other. He agreed that you cannot change to past but you have the power to change the future. You might not be able to influence and bring about changes in your partner but you can certainly change yourself. These changes might appear more accepted and be appealing to the partner. What's needed of you is to change your impulse reactions. I do not expect you to become too submissive to your partner but to be adjusting yourself for a more satisfying and conflict free relationship.

Afreen loved you and she did not leave you at her own wish, whims and fantasies but it was to save you from being decapitated or sure death. She has asked you to settle down in life, so do we both want. We still feel that you need to establish harmony and synergy between you, us and your future wife. Love is an ongoing process and efforts to sustain life. Both the partners must physically and emotionally be engaged with one another to establish these moments of love and continuity of the family. Your mother wants to see you a happy man before she departs. This is emotional blackmail Papa. This is a tough situation. I have learned it myself. Nothing is more annoying for me to think that I should learn to love again, just leave me alone and let me process my feelings, heal and make decisions for future relationships. Just support whatever work of self-discovery and healing, I am doing. If Afreen would have cheated me, I would have accepted your words immediately but NO, NOT NOW. I respect her sentiments and your affection to me but I don't think, I will fall in love again till some miracles happen.

I have got to learn a better way of coping with this. I am once bitten in love so twice shy in love.

22

The gap between Afreen and Manzoor was widening with each day passing. She was being abused physically almost every day on this pretext or other. She was getting afraid that she was going to have physical harm like injury etc. There were threats, pressures or forces to have sex. Even her son was a victim of domestic violence. This violence was not only a physical abuse, it was sexual, financial and emotional as well. For quite sometime Afreen suffered in silence being severely afraid of Manzoor harming or killing her.

Afreen's father always said that her marriage was an arranged marriage and Afreen always said that it was forced on her. She and Manzoor never even went out together. Afreen knew inside herself that she was only becoming his wife under coercion and domestic physical violence but she would never become his beloved as she didn't love him.

The most afterthought secret of her life was that she did few suicide attempts but she couldn't succeed.

In her words, "My family never knew about the abuse until I was in Hospital. My family only realized that something was not right with me when I was in the hospital. My parents and my brothers were in Lucknow and Manzoor didn't bother to inform them. They spoke with a hospital social worker who told them the story of her suicide attempts and physical beating mercilessly by Manzoor. They all reached Mumbai and had the first hand information from Manzoor. Afreen didn't speak a word about Manzoor but her eyes were saying the entire story.

23

Varun was surfing on net and found Afreen live. Afreen was an important romantic figure of his past. This was Varun's first and last love. He was confused for whether he would nudge her or no. It was almost ten years, they parted on relationship. He couldn't resist and got connected to Afreen. This renewed connection brought to mind the passion and enthusiasm of youth. For quite some time, there was silence on both ends. Both were at loss of words and also in dilemma of "was it wrong to have a texting relationship? Where would we draw the line? What was the line that would determine that this was an inappropriate relationship? Typically both the partners were in considerable pain and they wanted to heal their relationship and build the trust back.

The silence was broken at last.

Varun   - Hi Afreen, how are you? It was a pleasant surprise to find you on line and an unstoppable desire to hear you.

Afreen   - Hi Varun, I am good. How have you been for these long years?

Varun   - I am good too, busy with same routine of Clarks Awadh. Generating business improving the services of the hotel and showing that typical artificial and lifeless smiles.

Afreen   - Varun, I am sorry for all the hardships, torture you have undergone because of me. Actually my father took the reactions of their relatives, neighbours way more seriously than our feelings. He was always telling me about the loss of face in his respective societies if we would have done inter-faith marriage.

Varun   - Yeah, but it was ten years back. I have practically forgotten that.

Afreen   - Please take care of yourself and your family and keep in touch. I am normally on line between 4pm to 6pm as Manzoor is out in his office.

Varun   - Ok. I'll.

Interesting part of their discussion was that they both pretended to be happy in their lives and none disclosed anything about their families. Varun felt satisfied after understanding that Afreen was happy in her family but absolutely disappointed for not talking to her for a longer time. Same was the feeling, Afreen realized. Varun kept on trying to connect with Afreen but that was the last conversation. He tried daily at the appointed time but he couldn't get through.

24

Afreen was shell shocked with the attitude of her husband, Manzoor specially after sudden death of her son. Manzoor was always cursing her for their son's death as if Afreen has planned his murder after inflicting some germs of Pneumonia and Diarrhea. She had reached a point of no return and to get rid of this painful and unfortunate life. She planned to leave Manzoor with or without divorce knowing pretty well the emotional reality of a painful struggle.

The dreaded word DIVORCE in a way was providing a little solace to her. It can take months, if not years to reach a point to seek a divorce finally. As a woman who was in a toxic marriage, would at least inhale some fresh air from this sinless world. Every time she felt alone, every time she felt that her marriage was getting worse, every time she felt that nobody understood what she was going through including her own people, she turned to Allah whom she believed that he alone could either make her life peaceful or at least facilitate an end to her marriage and beginning of a new relationship something better.

She felt extremely shocked to understand and experience that Manzoor considered this physical and emotional abuse as Normal. Could be many Muslim males were also of the same thought of school. She did admit that even she owed the responsibility of this mess but it was out of her emotional failure due to a failed relationship with Varun but she at least expected Manzoor to give her some more time to heal and come out of that but he reacted and his reactions were all spontaneous without even a time delay of one second to think. Afreen was again in dilemma whether she should get a divorce or not. It was solely up to her to choose. She didn't know what to expect from her future, what were her options? Or what did she plan to do with life? Since she didn't have a road map and she never wanted to act on impulses, she turned to Allah, "Allah, I seek your guidance by virtue of your knowledge ....You have power, I have none. And you know, I know not. Allah, please help me and show me the way."

For few moment, she viewed Manzoor as a wicked man but next moment, she thought that he was simply a flawed human being just like her but persistent turbulence of life and death of her son didn't allow her to rethink continuity of her husband and wife relation and she decided after praying God that she would leave him, divorce or no divorce.

For Afreen even in deeply unhappy situations, there were still few moments of small happiness, little joys and pleasant memories, things to think back to and smile abort. Varun's memories were not completely erased off. She was able to just throw out the feelings of tenderness and compassion and to feel apathetic.

Afreen first tried to get some employment in the marketing division of multinational company, she got the job offer also but due to her ongoing domestic problems the company refused her the job. She then talked to her father to return to Lucknow but was told to adjust with her family as it was her family, her people. "There is a limit for everything Ammi, Abba, I am fed up with all this crap, Abba you can't say, it's my life and my family matter."

Nasir revolted against his father. He told him that religion is only a way of life and depends how you perceive others like Hindus, Christians, Jews etc. Ultimately they all are human beings created by one God, call him with different names. We all have seen Afreen and Varun in a narrow perspective. Abba, you married Afreen to Manzoor because Varun didn't agree to convert to Islam but at the same time, he never asked Afreen to convert to Hinduism. What great difference, Varun would have made after converting to Islam? There are many Hindu and Christian people who converted to Islam for the convenience of their marriages and once married, they are doing the same traditional things of their respective faiths as they were doing before conversion. Similarly there are Muslims married to Hindus girls who are not forcing them to follow Islam completely and they are all happy.

What we have done to Afreen, our sister, our blood, nothing except converting her to a mere skeleton. Iqbal though agreeing word to word with Nasir, didn't accept his mistake. Nasir told his father that we should have had a little more patience for acceptance. All religions have some values and spiritual aims at their core. Only the practices and traditions differ. We need to inculcate this basic understanding in all of us and help to see each of the religions as just one way to the spiritual enlightenment.

I will get Afreen home whether you like it or don't Abba. Heart to heart Iqbal loved his daughter and agreed to stand against anyone who didn't agree with Nasir, Be them be relatives or neighbours.

Nasir thanked Allah to remove Myopia from his father's eyes as he could see some logic in his thoughts and actions. He initiated the process of divorce for his daughter.

25

A conference of The Federation of Hotel and Restaurant Association of India (FHRAI) was organized in Hotel SUN and SAND in MUMBAI and Varun was nominated by Clarks Group of Hotels to represent them. FHRAI is mostly committed to the interests of providing the service of Hospitality community. As the main authentic voice of the hospitality Industry in India, FHRAI engages mainly with the Central and State Governments on a multiple issues like taxation, legal commitments and also for effective redressal for its members.

Many issues such as high incidence of taxes, indirect taxes like VAT, SERVICE TAX, LUXURY TAX, High Real Estate cost, development of skilled manpower and longer breakeven period were discussed and the decisions take to seek help from statutory bodies. The conference was attended by close to 200 delegates. This conference was for two consecutive days. One fine evening when Varun was in Infinity Mall of Andheri, to a Pharmacy Shop to get some pills for his diabetes, he suddenly saw a woman in Salwar Kameez, face half veiled. She was looking a familiar personality but seeing her under a veil, he hesitated for a moment but suddenly the breeze of the fan, helped him to see the complete face. Oh God, that really was a sticky situation of Varun. He was feeling excited and miserable at the same time. He thought of meeting her but again meeting Afreen would be like playing with fire. He saw her online almost four years back. She was looking pale and tired. There was unusual lightness of skin colour as compared to her normal complexion, a sign of Anemia. Varun studied somewhere that paleness can be a nonlife, threatening manifestation of emotions such as fear or severe Anemia. She was also there to get some of the medicines.

Afreen had a lively mind, intelligent and was always interested in doing lot of different things. The girl with ambition with that cute smile was life of every party or meetings. She was full of life and energy. She was gorgeous with a bubbly personality but what Varun could see was a skeleton wrapped with little mass and insufficient blood. There were few dark circles below her eyeballs and was looking so frail.

At the beginning, it was Varun's sheer will power and courage, he called out for Afreen with the name just the moment, she was going out of the shop after fetching her medicines. Afreen just took a second to place him. After exchanging few pleasantries, Varun asked her for a cup of Coffee in the Food Court of the Mall. She agreed with no resistance and they both occupied a corner table of the Food Court.

It was not easy to know how and what to talk to Afreen and have a proper conversation with her as talking about the past, break-up or relationship had a high risk of becoming depressed for both of them, but since communication was essential so Varun was trying to hide all his emotions.

Varun   - Afreen, you do not look healthy today. Are you Ok?

Afreen   - I am Ok. I wasn't well last week.

Varun   - You have lost on weight.

Afreen   - Yes, a bit. Ok Varun, now tell me about you and your family.

Varun   - I am good. I lost my father two years back. Mummy is fine. My sisters are all married and settled in Delhi.

Afreen was surprised, Varun didn't speak a word about his wife or kids.

Afreen   - You didn't say anything about your wife or kids?

Varun   - I haven't married Afreen. I met Nasir last week, they are all Ok, at your place except Nasir had some arguments with your Abba but now everything is cool there. You tell me about you and your family.

Afreen broke down and specially after knowing that Varun didn't marry.

Afreen   - I am going through a tough period, Varun. The day, I came to stay with Manzoor, he has never proved to be a husband and I have never been able to prove myself as his wife. Today, we are at the threshold of being separated.

She continued.... I did become a mother of a son under forced sexual encounter with my so called husband, in fact it was a cruel rape. I even lost my son as he was not given a proper medication on time.

Varun   - Oh, my God, you have gone through all this but Nasir never told me.

Afreen   - I only told all of them not to inform you anything about me.

Varun   - That's so unfortunate and is like, I could do nothing to change the situation. Now since you have decided to leave Manzoor, don't grieve for that relationship and feel relieved. You are free to do things, most people prevented you to do. If you are planning to build your career, there is no one to disappoint you. Share a sense of humour.

Afreen   - Varun, when it comes to regret, there is nothing like a failed relationship including my husband Manzoor. I, as a woman, am more to be blamed but tell me Varun what is it about me that I could have done differently?

Varun   - Under the circumstances, you have not done anything which a normal woman like you, would have not done. Honest reflection and revelation after a relationship can never be bad thing.

Afreen   - Hmm

Varun   - Now focus on the positiveness and turn your energies to getting with your life rather than regressing.

Afreen - Why didn't you settle in life? Why didn't you get married? I wrote a note to you and requested you to fulfill my this wish.

Varun - To be honest, I didn't find another Afreen to replace the first one. To where is question? As Krishna once told Radha why he didn't marry Radha. He said, to marry, you need two people but we are one as you are within me and I am within you so the question of marriage doesn't rise.

Afreen - You have answer for everything.

Varun - What's your plan for future?

Afreen - You know as much as I know. I'll not beg anyone for anything. Keeping my dignity is my prime essential duty. I am reborn not to take pains. My parting advice to you Varun, now is, please have your own family. My life is filled with uncertainties. I am not sure whether we would meet again but for my sake, let me not live in a guilt that Varun didn't marry because I left him half way.

They both parted ways, unknown and indifferent to each other to an unknown destiny.

They had no regrets for each other.

26

"Muslim men can divorce their wife or wives for any reason at all or for no reason. All that is necessary is for him to pronounce the Arabic word TALAQ which means divorce or I divorce you. After pronouncing the TALAQ three times either consecutively all at once or spread out over a period of time, the divorce is considered to be final and irrevocable. The man cannot again remarry a woman for whom he has issued triple TALAQ."

Manzoor waited for three months and wrote a letter to Afreen in few words "I divorce you" three times. That is it all took. Her 5 years of marriage came to an end with that letter and next moment Afreen became a divorced woman. She was not even asked, she was not even present when he wrote the word "DIVORCE" what kind of a one sided unfair divorce was this? Most Muslims in India follow family laws that are governed by their religion. This practice then by Muslims known as triple Talaq or triple divorce was most controversial.

It was ridiculous that a Muslim man to divorce his wife is allowed by merely uttering these words by mouth, by mail or even over Skype or text message. Afreen never wanted to contest this way of Talaq but since she wanted to get rid of that rotten relationship, she didn't protest or did police complaint or she opted for any other legal options.

She coolly walked off the relationship and left Mumbai to come to Lucknow with her brother Nasir. She didn't even ask for return of the MEHER, the guarantee money of the Nikah.

After reaching to her parents place, she never went to any religious school and never wore a veil. Her father wanted her daughter to think herself as free Indian first, not just as Muslim woman.

Little later than a month, she got the divorce letter and she declined to discuss the reason for the divorce with anybody. "Some women are strong and can handle divorce. Some are weak." Afreen was the strongest.

Afreen resumed at Christian College, Lucknow as a lecturer and it became her daily routine to go to the college and come back home. Sit quietly. She was still recovering. Meanwhile Manzoor got married to his own cousin.

27

Iqbal when he was seeing his daughter in sick tiring and quiet conditions, he was always getting the shock of his life beyond imagination. "My tiny little girl that has slept on my chest for days and years has come to this pathetic condition. He started crying loudly. Memories of her childhood, her presence in parties in and out of their home, her elementary school plays and her going to school in uniform, all started appearing in front of his eyes like a flash back of time. What have I not done that I needed to do for her? Will she look back on her childhood with positive memories? Was my decision to marry her to Manzoor right? These questions caused me to evaluate the father I have been, what I have been what would I regret if I didn't make some changes fast?

I have committed a blunder and made her life a living hell but I don't have to carry it for a life time. I have to take corrective action and heal my guilt or crime. Today I regret being so critical of the views, Afreen expressed about her relationship with Varun and I as stupid person on earth only listened to me like a Frog of a well who always thinks that he is the king of the world but actually he is only the king of well. All along I lived in the illusion that my daughter's marriage to a Muslim man Manzoor was the truth of world and Allah's verdict to me. I didn't throw away that attitude. My daughter Afreen remained hung on every word, her father uttered whether it be encouraging or discouraging. My daughter has developed that bitterness between father and daughter relationship and specially when I tried different antics including kidnapping Varun and trying to kill him. This bitterness has been part of her life for almost over ten years. I now realize that as a father I gave her everything she wanted. I made her the queen of the house. Somehow, she agreed to marry Manzoor against her wishes and her marriage failed in large part due to her husband never being able to satisfy her constant need for his complete attention and his lack of interest in Afreen.

No matter how old Afreen is today or how many mistakes, I must have made in the past, I'll improve my relationship with her moving forward. I may have become late but I would correct her way of life and bring her into the main stream. I will apologize to my daughter.

Afreen has always been a rock throughout all these years but deep down, I know she is hollow because of all the problems of her relationship with Varun and her marriage to Manzoor but I would make her happy at any price.

Iqbal one day after a big thought left a note at the reading/study table of Afreen;

My dear Afreen,

Your Abba is extremely painful and apologize for all the sufferings/pain/trauma my little darling daughter has gone through. There are certain things which can't be undone now but your Abba promises that he would only do right things as Allah advises but he would ensure that my daughter will not have even a single tear in her eyes.

Your Abba sincerely apologizes once again. Afreen cried the whole night after reading her father's note. She didn't know, how to react. After she stopped crying, she wrote;

My very dear Abba,

I forgive you for not always being there when I needed you and for not being the dad, I expected. I forgive the mistakes, you made. It may seem like, it's too late it is not. There is still so much time to move forward. Abba, I also had both inspiring highs and crushing lows of life. I have become a mechanical creature.

I would always love you Abba.

Next day, they were just two to forget everything of the past. Abba hugged his daughter after so many years.

28

In India Govt. employees and employees of private sector companies of all ranks are appointed for the life time till they retire from service after reaching the age of 60 years or more depending on the caliber of the employees. It is sometimes next to impossible to remove them due to the complicated procedures of removal and the constitutional protection given to them or they are protected by unions or associations. The people in private sectors do not have that guarantee.

Varun's case in clarks was different. He was working there since beginning and was an asset to the organization. Clarks Group of Hotels opened their marketing office in Florida, USA to increase their international market and also to create their brand in USA. In addition to the hospitality business Clarks also wanted to increase their market base for silk sarees and other silk production and around USA which was their main business before they entered into Hospitality industry. Who could be better person other than Varun to head their international branch in U.S.

Varun was redesignated as General Manager Marketing & Export and transferred initially for five years at Florida office. A big sendoff was given to him to share his experience at Clarks Avadh with his colleagues. His achievements were lauded by the Front Office Manager who said, " Welcome all. We are gathered here at this special occasion of farewell party of our senior colleague Mr.Varun Sharma who has been promoted as General Manager and posted at our new marketing office at Florida, USA. I am here to express my feelings on behalf of all of us to him for the time he has been with us in this company and appreciate and congratulate him for his promotion and marvelous achievements of Varun. It is a sad moment to say him goodbye after working with him for a nice long 19 years but are also proud for his tenure and future endeavour. His great achievements would inspire all of us to be a role model like him. Thanks a million Varun for your support, help and a happy working environment. We all wish you all success in life. Thank you." Varun thanked everyone present for the kind words on behalf of Clarks Group of Hotels. In his farewell speech, he said that it was a nice journey with Clarks and all of you which would be a memory for me always. This is the organization that taught me everything about my responsibility. If you are true and sincere about your duties and responsibilities, Clarks will have no limit for rise.

I would like to say you all a goodbye for everything especially the love and care you have given me and wish you all a bright career and peaceful life. Thank you very much. Varun took over his new assignment and got himself accustomed to the new environment and working conditions in U.S. He understood the concept of meetings which are very common irrespective of making big decisions or not. Yes, by his sheer hard work and public relations, he gave a good business in Hospitality and silk products.

The management of Clarks Group of Hotels forgot that Varun's posting was only for five years which was further extended for five years and he remained in U.S. for close to ten years.

29

The students can't excel in their life in absence of a good teacher. The success of any college or institution depends on the quality of education. Afreen became the Head of the Department, HOD of Humanities Science in 10 years rising from a Associate Lecturer. Her main contribution as HOD was for ....

- Preparing syllabus for Classes
- Preparing for examinations
- Meeting students outside the class for help
- Integrating new learning technics into latest ones
- Supervising the research work of graduate students.
- Participating in various departmental faculty meetings

Afreen had deep passion for teaching, complex problem solving ability, Persuasion ability for senior students. She had good communication skill and its monitoring power. Altogether Afreen was one of the role models of entire teaching fraternity of Christian College. She worked close to 15 years and took voluntary retirement to work full time for her one NGO, called Muslim Education Trust, MET. It was a voluntary educational NGO which was established in 1989 to work for the betterment of minorities giving top priority to education as its objective.

Afreen worked hard since its inception to bring about social and educational change in the present conditions of the community by awarding scholarships to needy students in pursuit of higher professional education. The main objective of her trust was to work for the advancement of education for Science and Technology and management. She also arranged loans and scholarships to deserving students for higher studies and research work in field of Medicines, Engineering and other professional allied fields. Since its beginning, Afreen was able to organize too many Talent search and competitions and in opening new schools in slum areas of the capital city, Lucknow.

Afreen specially focused and worked hard for the upliftment and betterment of the girls by providing them education, shelter and clothings across the city. She took good care of girls to improve and make their lives better. She insisted upon all girls including the underprivileged ones to be educated as Education was one of the most important medium that will enhance their standard of living. She was being supported by the team of teachers, doctors, trainers and other volunteers.

In the process, she forgot everything including Varun and only remembered her NGO with her selfless service.

30

Time and tide wait for nobody and there is no one so powerful that he or she can stop the march of time. Afreen was divorced and hurt and her marriage to Manzoor was already dissolved. She had also experienced a disappointing relationship with Varun so not all the time but yes, sometimes, she felt intensely painful life not only for herself but for Varun too. She never ever imagined to be loved again so she had started focusing on her own interests. Even though she had a painful divorce with series of disappointing incidences like losing her son, she trusted Varun. Actually she wanted to take care of Varun at this age.

She did not need a man to make her happy physically, but she wanted Varun to share their lives with. The whole concept of romantic relationship had a different meaning for this stage of life. She was thinking about Varun to share mutual interests, common dreams and laughters. Obviously she had no goal of having children.

Varun was a lazy man after retirement. He had nothing to do except a walk in the morning and reading daily newspaper line to line, word to word including matrimonial columns not for him but in general just like that but there was not a single moment or a day, he did not remember Afreen. Afreen was like a fairy only to be imagined but not to be touched. Yes, she could be felt in mind and heart. What he wanted from Afreen was that he should feel appreciated, feel desirable and honoured. It was to ensure his feelings for conversation, companionship and enjoy each other's company. Whether it was a residual love connection with Afreen or was she still becoming so difficult to be discarded.

Yes in spite of the age beyond love of Hormones, they both had not given up on love. Varun was optimistic about the prospects for love in his life. According to Varun, this might take a form of marriage, a committed relationship or just walking down the streets holding hands together. Love could be part of his life at any age and was willing to be brave, confident and open to possibilities and also willing to take a chance on letting love into their hearts once again. He was developing an intense love for Afreen excluding the sexual relationship which he was not sure of the capacity and capability of both the partners.

Varun decided to meet Afreen and explore a selfless love relationship with her. While he was struggling with the idea of hope or no hope, somebody knocked his door. When Varun opened the door, he found his dear friend, old school and college mate, Nasir after so many years. Varun was pleasantly shocked and Nasir was so happy to see each other. Both of them had a long and inseparable hug creating a challenging noise of their ribs. Both had grey all over.

Nasir told Varun that Afreen was complaining about you. She was saying that when Afreen was young and beautiful, Varun always found her wherever she was, including his search twice, once on line and second time in a Mall in Mumbai. HE is a cheater as he is not bothered about her now. THE SELFISH OLD DUDE. Varun gave Nasir a cryptic smile and promised to see Afreen in a day or so. He would also meet Abba, Afreen's father and talk to him. Nasir told him that Abba has grown old but he is active and has a very sharp memory.

Next day, Varun and Afreen both nearly bumped into each other at Afreen's place. Afreen glanced out of window and noticed an overweight, gray-haired man, sucking hard on a cigarette and looking as if he had the weight of the entire world on his shoulders. Varun walked in the drawing room. He didn't smile which actually unnerved Afreen. She was stunned of the physical change in him. Afreen as usual in anger like their old days, asked Varun when did he start smoking? He was caught on the wrong foot and started hiding his emotions and fear of Afreen's firing. Afreen could feel that Varun was miserable, utterly miserable and it was clear that he was a troubled man in a very bad situation.

Varun, you haven't taken care of yourself and I won't allow you to play with your own life. You have become irresponsible with smoking and what not. He smilingly confessed by saying, "only smoking." She told Varun to go to marriage counseling and guidance find some job, lose some weight and start looking after yourself physically. Varun thought that he would speak this and that but he couldn't open his mouth even once in front of Afreen. The only word with great courage, he could utter was that "I missed you Afreen all these years which her father was able to hear as he entered the drawing room then."

Iqbal called all his sons and daughters-in-law to discuss Afreen's future. He told his people that as a father of Afreen at the centre of controversy tell you all that she is a matured woman so she can marry Varun. I should have done it before but I was made and was in a cobweb following certain unnecessary tenets of Islam which nobody has clarified as yet. Who are we to force them? Today also Varun and Afreen die for each other. Afreen could have eloped with Varun many years ago but she respected our sentiments and Varun supported her all along. Varun had profusely accepted her love for him then and now. I have already had harrowing experience on the controversy over their alleged relationship.

Akbar, the eldest son and brother of Afreen told his father that it is HARAAM for a Muslim woman to marry a Non-Muslim man regardless of love and feelings. Nasir interfered that these are old civilization sayings which are irrelevant today. Humanity is the best religion so I have no problem in marrying Afreen to Varun. There are many instances that Muslim women have married Hindus and they are happy and none of the Islamic clerics are raising fingers on them just because they are rich guys. I would support Afreen and Varun, come what may.

Varun who was silent all along and listening to all said, Abba, I believe that God created us with the diversity of race, religion, language and belief to get to know one another, respect one another and uphold our collective human dignity and I also believe that Islam is a religion of peace and mercy and I respect the sanctity of all human life, the taking of which is among the gravest of all his sins. I have never insisted upon Afreen changing to Hinduism and so is she never asked me to convert so I still feel that none of us has to convert and get married. The same issue was there when we both were in our twenties and the same is still existing. Nothing has changed in so many years except that Abba has become mild and moderate but I could respect Abba and would not create a situation when he becomes victim of circumstances like mudslinging, abuses from the community especially from the hard line Muslim clerics who would not listen to his logics.

Afreen said I am not now of a marriageable age who could become a problem for the family. I am also not depending financially or socially on you all. My life from last 35 years has not been liveable even for one day so I reject the proposal of my marriage with Varun outright. If any one of you feels otherwise, I will also quit this home immediately.

Varun interrupted and said Mr.Khan, this time he didn't use word Abba. I would not marry Afreen so violation of any of the Islamic customs, rituals, rules and laws will not happen. Secondly, we have both crossed that age that our marriage for producing kids to please Allah, will not be in anyway violation of Hinduism and Islam. Since both of us are in love and do not think to live without each other, I would suggest that I would take care of all the needs of Afreen to live a healthy and respectful life. Afreen would stay with me as she cannot take even the minor shock and I would be her guardian and she would be my guardian. She would stay at my house and will not be like modern day live-in-relationship. I would respect her religion and she would respect mine. She will carry out 5 times prayers as usual in my house and I will continue with my religious aspirations. We will stay together till we both are alive. Now if the same is acceptable to you all, I will make arrangements to take Afreen to my house and if the same is not acceptable to you, then also I will take her. What we both didn't do in the past, we'll do it now.

Everybody agreed and Varun took his girlfriend home in a week's time without any celebration or noise. They became one soul in two bodies since then and started living with a feeling as they knew each other for centuries.

31

It is generally accepted that true love comes to those who wait and this lovely bubbly couple of Afreen and Varun has waited longer than most. The couple was displaying passion and excitement like any newlyweds (They were never married) setting out on their new lives together. Life is for living and loving so Afreen loved Varun and Varun did more. Varun always said that his ambitions were to make Afreen happy with a beaming smile. "I want to give her the best day of her life every day. She is my dream girl." Afreen used to say that Varun has got marvelous eyes and she couldn't resist looking into them. If Varun can just colour his grey hair, I can find my original young Varun in him now. He was almost a forgotten hero but she is surprised by how many feelings quickly grew for him. He is more loving when he got older. "He gets the glow on his face when I draw him closer to me" said Afreen. Varun responded, "I was resigned to being alone on my own forever and ever and when Afreen agreed to be with me, my life started again. Everybody deserves love and sometimes it is right there in front of you. You've just got to take that step and I have just done that only. Afreen is the love of my life."

Varun suggested to Afreen that it was just right to wait for years to be with you. Varun hugged Afreen and kissed her. Afreen realized that the old man still had the same josh in him and asked him to shave off his beard and moustaches. For both of them, there were few surprises in their love life like surprise kisses, watching the sunset together or enjoying old Hindi movies, Holding hands or taking the time to express specific things, watching each other without the other person knowing about have added spice to their love life. Evening drives anywhere and meals at good restaurants was another pass time for the couple.

When it used to take a little extra efforts, romance made them healthier, happier with fulfilling relationship. Biological, demographical and psychological factors have still not affected these two people to form romantic relationship. They were both reasonably sexually active.

One fine evening, Afreen was staring at Varun which he was not aware of. He was busy planning a trip together with Afreen, what caught her eye was how he was getting hotter even as he was getting older. He looked smoldering hot even when he is mid 5th decade of his life. Looking around she discovered that man who not only carried his age very well but his sex appeal too had gone up a few notches than when he was younger. She drew his attention and told him that Varun, your emotions are increasing and suggesting next level of love which I think, I can't afford. Varun was quick to explain, "Yes, I agree that both of us have reached an age where it wasn't quite like as it would have been in our late 20's, 30's or even 40's but we have to take the best use of our available resources. Afreen caught hold of his hands and said, I am still not recovered and I needed you now and forever. Varun, tell me why you still like me so much asked Afreen. Varun said, "I see a thousand roses in your face, a million stars twinkling in your eyes and the love, the beauty of your being. You are just made for me. Yes, they were romantically so involved that night that they didn't sleep till morning when the maid rang the doorbell to tell them that it was already 8 AM.

Another evening when Afreen was in kitchen doing some cooking and Varun followed her there and wanted to share some of Afreen's domestic work and he realized that the participation in domestic work leads to intimacy and more sex in relationship. "Varun told Afreen that even without make up and faint lipstick, you are looking beautiful. Afreen is a human being so she surrendered to his charm and they united in body and soul and they had no regrets for this.

32

India has to offer much more to a traveler if we do not restrict our vision to Mumbai, Delhi, Bangalore and Goa etc. Keeping this in mind, Varun planned a trip to two small tours of Rajasthan to see a very different side of India. Varun flew from Lucknow to Jaipur and stayed at Clarks Amer with Afreen where he showed the entire property and the areas which were once submerged in water and sand in a devastating flood of 19th July 1981. They both drove to explore the two neighbouring towns of Ajmer and Pushkar.

His first priority was to show the most important and prominent spot in Ajmer, The Ajmer Shariff Dargah. It is also called Khwaja Gareeb Nawas Dargah named after the Sufi saint Hazrat Khwaja Moinuddin Chishty. The dargah is extremely holy to people from all faiths and religions as they come to pray to Khwaja Ji and seek his blessings. The faith in the dargah is so immense that it is believed that if you pray with a clean and pure heart, your wish shall be granted. The main shrine inside or the tomb where Khwaja Ji rests, is the inner sectrum where you pray however there is also a mosque with plenty of space outside to pray sit or mediate. Afreen covered her till shoulders and Varun covered his head according to the protocol and prayed inside the tomb area.

Afreen also noticed the beautiful Mughal architecture in the Masjid area in addition to the devotional blessings. He was very happy and thankful to Varun for his priority. She was aspiring to visit Ajmer Shariff for a very long time as a long cherished dream.

They then drove to Pushkar. Both the towns are very close to each other just 40 Kms distance to cover in less than one hour. Both these towns attract a lot of people because of their temples and religious shrines. India is a country where faith and religion play an important role for the people. Both the towns have hotels. They stayed in TAJ, a beautiful property of Taj Group of Hotels, surrounded by beautiful hills, peace and tranquility and with assured some top notch service and tasteful luxury. The food served here is grand affair highlighting local regional flavor and all other five star facilities. The best part was its situation in between Ajmer and Pushkar and second best was Camel Safari in Pushkar.

Pushkar is known for its famous Camel fair. More than this is its claim to fame is that it is home to the oldest Brahma temple in the world. The temple is unique and located near the Pushkar lake which is holy site. There are plenty of shops and street vendors selling everything from clothes to knickknacks next to the temple. It's very small town and the most prominent feature is lake. You can enjoy the sunset in the evening at the Pushkar lake and walk across the other side by 7 PM and witness a beautiful Aarti. An aarti is a Hindu religion ritual of worship and this particular is done by the lake side where a priest lights a huge lamp and everyone chants prayers and mantras and the entire experience is just beautiful. There are few other temples also like Savitri temple dedicated to the first wife of Brahma. It is situated at 300 steps while walking or taking a cable car. Afreen enjoyed the ride up and down which was stunning as you can get beautiful views of the hills and of course a fantastic view of Pushkar. They both participated in the lake Aarti and got Prasad from the priest.

While returning from Jaipur, they stopped at Kishangarh which is famous for its 18th Century School of the Rajasthan style of Indian paintings. Afreen purchased an expensive RADHA KRISHNA painting of 18th Century design and few Mughal art paintings of 17th Century for their house. The master artist must have been largely responsible for transmitting the romantic and religious passions of both Afreen and Varun. In the evening, they reached Hotel Clarks Amer again for their two days stay.

Jaipur is a demanding yet captivating tourist destination that is full of extremes from opulent and lavish palaces to grinding daily poverty. A two days stay in Jaipur is often sufficient to visit all the major tourist sites.

Next day morning after a tasteful breakfast at Clarks Amer, Afreen and Varun first visited City Palace, Jantar Mantar, Hawa Mahal (Palace of winds) and watched sunset at the sun temple. They had lovely typical vegetarian lunch at the very oldest vegetarian restaurant LMB (Laxmi Mistan Bhandar) and returned to Clarks Amer late evening fully tired.

Second day was very exciting for both of them including an elephant ride at Amer Fort and evening for shopping in the local markets. Afreen was too excited to see the stuff in the markets. She purchased ten typical Rajasthani Lahariya Silk Sarees and a lot of dress material for herself. Varun purchased two pairs of typical Rajasthani MOZARIES (Shoes). He gifted a beautiful Mughal gown to Afreen which she was searching in Lucknow but couldn't get. So a beautiful Muslim girl in a typical Rajasthani gown was looking stunning and tempting for Varun for a mischief.

Finally they landed in Sanganer for blue potteries and printed bed sheets. Afreen was more than happy for visiting Ajmer Shariff, Pushkar and nice shopping at Jaipur.

Next day morning, they flew back to Lucknow after a very satisfying trip. Varun called it a nice honeymoon trip.

33

Time leapt by year by year and then five years. It has never been that Varun and Afreen have not slept without holding hands even for one night. Everything in life was going on well until one evening when Afreen has gone for some grocery shopping for home and it started raining with thunders and lightening, bringing the temperature of Lucknow to 10^0C. She didn't carry an umbrella as the sky was clear that time. By the time she returned, she was completely drenched with chilled water rain water.

After the dinner, they went to sleep. A little before midnight she had a bout of cough and cold with fever of 101^0F. Varun gave her some cough syrup and Crocin for fever and she slept after some time. Suddenly Varun felt that she was having shortness of breath. Varun was also able to hear a whistling or wheezy sound coming out of her chest with the breath and she was feeling quite uncomfortable. Within one hour Afreen was admitted in King George Hospital in emergency ward. The first examination by doctors revealed that she had asthma attack, a chronic condition that causes inflammation and narrowing of bronchial tubes, the passageways that allows air to enter and leave lungs. She was complaining of constant coughing, breathing difficulty, chest tightness and whistling sound while breathing.

Series of tests were conducted by the most experienced doctors of King George Hospital and it was detected that Afreen has suffered a devastating asthma attack that could be life threatening. She was advised minimum of seven days hospitalization and during all these days, a regular visits by doctors, nurses, respiratory specialists and even the cleaning staff were there in full attendance on round the clock basis. Every single one of them was treating Afreen with such professionalism, kindness and dignity.

On the last day, she was to be discharged but before discharging her, the doctors wanted to conduct few more final tests to ascertain that she was fit to be relieved from the hospital. Unfortunately, the sugar level in her blood showed an exorbitant value of 500 mg/dl and Afreen was also turning semi-unconscious. The doctors refused to discharge her. They advised Varun to keep Afreen under observation for one more week and treat her high level of blood sugar. They told him that high sugar levels slowly erode the ability of cells in our pancreas to make insulin and its continuance in body can harm Kidneys, Vision loss, heart attacks or strokes, weaken immune system and much more. Varun got worried for Afreen. He was with her days and nights but how many more nights? How much longer would he watch his Afreen, his love, his best friend struggle against this merciless disease that was destroying her every day? How could someone so healthy and energetic has fallen victim to this monster of an illness?

Tragedy doesn't come alone or misfortunes never come singly proved true to Varun, Afreen was kept on regular dialysis. She started losing weight. Suspecting the hardening of heart artilleries, she was taken for stress test and echo test for heart for fatigue and fast breathing (panting). It was finally decided to carry out Angiography and then Angioplasty if needed. Initially Afreen didn't agree for her heart operation but on continuous insistence from Varun, she agreed for. Varun was able to talk, to laugh and to encourage Afreen and could no longer let Afreen know that he was a worried man, yet still, Afreen could make out from his voice trembling with grief. Afreen gathered all the strength and courage within her and told Varun, "You are still the most important person in the world to me." "I won't leave you, I promise." "If you don't see me on to the bed, I could be in a chair or in the corridor or bathroom but I would be right back." "I won't leave you, I promise." She was constantly repeating this. Suddenly, Varun felt her arms around him, holding him as if Varun was a frightened child. He was holding on his tears for so long but could not hold them for long and he was only sobbing his head down resting on Afreen's hand and doctors were just consoling him.

The hospital management was able to find the Kidney donor who was asked to come to the hospital. It was then decided to transplant Kidneys first and then do the Angiography/Angioplasty. Varun was waiting for Afreen's organ donor surgery but the donor didn't turn up. Varun now was emotionally and physically exhausted. The doctors asked Varun to leave the room as he was beyond consolation. He came back after sometime and rested his body against her's. He was stroking her hair and face and was trying to feel her heartbeats with the rise and fall with each breath. He touched Afreen and all her sorrows came pouring out.

She was taken to the operation theatre for angiography and the results were quite disturbing so doctors took a decision of carrying out Angioplasty. During the operation itself, she got the heart stroke. The inevitable happened. She turned away from Varun's world and she, Afreen quietly died. Varun was numb. He was so shocked that he couldn't speak. For him love was a reason to live and the purpose is defeated.

34

Varun brought the dead body of Afreen from the hospital to his place and called Nasir and his brothers there. According to Varun by virtue of staying with Varun and following certain Hindu rituals and festivals, she has become part Hindu but basically to the large extent she maintained her Islamic identity and life by offering prayer five times. Varun didn't perform too elaborate Hindu rituals and left everything on Nasir and his family to decide.

According to Muslim clerics, Muslim community believes that the good deeds one done in life will yield entry into paradise on the day of judgment, also called the last day, when the world will be destroyed. Many Muslims believe that until the last day, the dead will remain in their tombs and those heading towards heaven will experience peace while those heading for hell will experience suffering.

As soon as the body was handed over to Nasir, all the Muslim people assembled there said, "INNA

LILLAHI WA INNA ILAYHI RAJI'UN (verify we belong to Allah and truly to him shall we return). The people closed Afreen's eyes and covered her with a clean sheet. A local Islamic community organization was contacted and they Varun and Nasir to identify funeral home. The body was washed by the female family of Nasir. They followed all Islamic rituals and put Afreen's body to rest in the grave and the grave was covered.

35

After Afreen's funeral Varun became all alone and kept saying always, "I just want to go, I just want to go with her."

He always woke up with Afreen, had morning walks with her. They were always together. He didn't eat properly and all his activities were now confined to his house. Whether he had a premonition or what, just one week before he called his legal expert and wrote his will that all his money and the big house would be given to Afreen's NGO. Varun also expired within six month without any symptoms of illness.

Nasir with the help of his friends cremated Varun with full Hindu traditions and rituals with full respect. Nasir cried bitterly after losing his sister and brother-in-law (supposedly).

36

This is the end of a story, my love story which has not died a natural death but has been killed by the thoughts, customs of fanatics from both Islamic community and hard liner Hinduism. They both wanted to live in a society which is free from ethno-religious conflicts and in society controlled by Humanity.

Varun and Afreen probably would at least have initiated and could see the light at the end of tunnel.

Characters

1) Varun

2) Afreen   - Varun's Girlfriend

3) Iqbal   - Afreen's Father

4) Akbar, Anwar,   - Afreen's Brothers
    Adil, Nasir

5) Manzoor   - Afreen's Husband

6) Mr.Gupta   - Clarks Managing Director

Other Books Published by Author